Pasó por Aquí

Series on the Nuevomexicano Literary Heritage

Edited by Genaro Padilla and Erlinda Gonzales-Berry

TIERRA AMARILLA

Stories of New Mexico
Cuentos de Nuevo Mexico

By SABINE R. ULIBARRI

Translated from the Spanish by
Thelma Campbell Nason

Introduction by Erlinda Gonzales-Berry

Albuquerque
UNIVERSITY OF NEW MEXICO PRESS

ISBN-13: 978-0-8263-1438-3
E-ISBN: 978-0-8263-2680-5

Illustrated by Kercheville

17 16 15 14 13 12 3 4 5 6 7 8

Library of Congress Cataloging-in-Publication Data

Ulibarrí, Sabine R.
[Tierra Amarilla. English & Spanish]
Tierra Amarilla: stories of New Mexico: cuentos de Nuevo Mexico/ by Sabine R. Ulibarrí: translated from the Spanish by Thelma Campbell Nason; introduction by Erlinda Gonzales-Berry; [illustrated by Kercheville].
p. cm.—(Pasó por aquí)
Contents: my wonderful horse—The stuffing of the Lord—The Frater Family—Get that straight—Forge without fire—Man without a name.
ISBN 0-8263-1438-4
1. Tierra Amarilla (N. M.)—Social life and customs—Fiction.
I. Title. II. Series.
PQ7079.2 U4T513 1993 93-1882
863—dc20 CIP

To the people about whom
the book is written

Dedico este libro
a mi Raza

FOREWORD

Tierra Amarilla. Yellow Land. The adjective evokes an erroneous concept of the small Spanish-American village whose name provides the title for this book. Green, not yellow, is the predominant color, for the town lies in a valley cradled in the pine-haired arms of New Mexico's high northern mountains. Equally deceptive is its appearance. Somnolent, unchanging, grown shabby with the years, it impresses the casual visitor as a relic from the past, a sanctuary from modern turbulence. Yet Tierra Amarilla recently exploded into national headlines with an armed raid on the county courthouse. There are indications, too, that this glare of publicity was not merely a transient flash, that the spotlight will focus again and again on this adobe village in its stream-stitched valley.

Tierra Amarilla has never been a peaceful place. The county seat of Río Arriba County whose crowding mountains and high plateaus are snow blocked in winter and isolated in summer, it developed stalwart individualists, proud men of action who lived by struggle. Its history is interwoven with the murky complex of legal and local battles over Spanish and Mexican land grants which, since 1854, have engendered in its people a sense of injustice, envy, and sometimes hatred.

The descendants of the first colonists, who still inhabit the area, are more Spanish than American. Part of the paradox of New Mexico is the fact that the Hispanic heritage becomes more ingrown and more intense the farther it is removed from its colonial source, the "New Spain" or Mexico of three centuries ago. Spanish is the universal speech; in many mountain villages, English is seldom heard. Isolated from the normal development of the mother tongue, this speech is replete with sixteenth-century forms now obsolete in other parts of the world. Like their progenitors, the people are profoundly Catholic. Catholicism, in the words of the author of this book, is a religion which may be worn either as a silken cloak or as a hair shirt. Many mountain people have chosen the latter garb, with the result that religious fanaticism is characteristic of the area. It is no accident that in these mountains lies the epicenter of the mystic Penitente brotherhood whose sanguinary rituals come to light only in the observances of Holy Week. Neither is it accidental nor irrelevant that barn burnings, fence cuttings, and occasional murders practiced by secret organizations preceded for many years the open violence of the Tierra Amarilla courthouse raid of June 1967.

This land and its people provide the background for both the stories in *Tierra Amarilla* and their author, Sabine Reyes Ulibarrí.

His forebears entered New Mexico centuries ago with that conquering wave of Spanish soldiers and settlers that swept from the high southwest-Castilian plateau of Extramadura over most of the New World. Ulibarrí grew up in Tierra Amarilla, steeped in its traditions and in the independent spirit of its isolation. The boy who rode the range on his father's ranch left the region, however, to study and travel in far places, from Europe to Latin America. Today he is a professor of Spanish literature in the University of New Mexico. His sensitivity to beauty, developed in those far-off days and distant mountains, plus an element of Spanish mysticism in his soul, made the writing of poetry inevitable. Two volumes, *Al Cielo Se Sube a Pie* and *Amor y Ecuador*, attest to his poetic ability and a critical study, *El Mundo Poético de Juan Ramón Jiménez*, to his appreciation of the great Spanish poet.

Perhaps because it was so different from his adult world, the Tierra Amarilla of his childhood always remained a vibrant reality in the mind of Sabine Ulibarrí. He fascinated his friends with its stories, like that of the legendary white stallion that roamed the mountains or the good and simple priest who kept the townspeople in helpless and agonized laughter during his stay among them. Some of his listeners insisted that he write these stories for two reasons. In the first place, they focus on a facet of American life that is passing with no hope of return. Also, it was felt that the profound Hispanicity of this part of the country should be represented by some literary work in the language. Since the stories were written, the light of recent events has revealed a third reason—the need for developing by every means possible an understanding of the region and its problems.

Most of the stories in this small collection are golden with the light of youth. They depict customs and traditions of a bygone

day. They portray foibles, injustices, and individuals from a boy's view. But underneath all of them runs a current of understanding, of empathy with the character of these strong, kindly, often violent inhabitants of the mountains of New Mexico.

To present to English-speaking America the cultural and aesthetic values these people have developed, I have translated the stories from their original Spanish. They are presented in this book in both languages, an appropriate form of publication in this, the only one of the United States of America which is officially bilingual.

Welcome, then, to Tierra Amarilla. Here you will meet the descendants of men and women whose fields and houses dotted the banks of New Mexican streams before either Jamestown or Plymouth Colony was established.

Thelma Campbell Nason

INTRODUCTION

It is fitting that Sabine Ulibarrí's *Tierra Amarilla* be included in the "Pasó por Aquí Series." It is a text that serves as a bridge between that phase of the *Nuevomexicano* literary tradition that literary historians today would call the contemporary "Chicano" period and that produced by the twentieth-century pioneer writers.[1] What Ulibarrí shares with earlier writers like Nina Otero Warren, Cleofas Jaramillo, Fabiola C de Baca, Fray Angelico Chavez, all of whom wrote in English, is a nostalgic vision of the past coupled with an urgent desire to document that past for posterity. His use of Spanish links him to the Chicano generation because, for this generation, "language became central to their discourse of cultural identity,

affirmation, and self-determination" (Gonzales-Berry, 8). I say this conscious of the fact that Ulibarrí prefers to not be called a Chicano writer. For him that term connotes a foregrounded agenda of social realism and a political ideology that he claims not to privilege in his own work. Also, his use of Spanish was probably motivated by more practical than ideological considerations; he wrote and first published *Tierra Amarilla* in Ecuador in 1964. The publication of this bilingual version in the United States in 1971, however, comes in the wake of the Chicano literary "boom."[2] At that moment, the publication of Spanish language works by bilingual Hispanics in this country was seen as a political statement, bold in its contestational stance and firm in its call for recognition of the cultural difference of *La Raza*. It is difficult, if not impossible, not to conceive of *Tierra Amarilla* as sharing in that spirit. With the dedication of *Tierra Amarilla* to "Mi Raza," Ulibarrí joins other writers of Mexicano-hispano origin in the political act of creating a space for the expression of their cultural and linguistic difference. Moreover, when Ulibarrí's subsequent works are published by Chicano presses (Justa, The Bilingual Press, Arte Público), he joins the brother- and sisterhood of Chicano literati—the engagé as well as those who would write to delect and entertain rather than to inspire revolutions. More importantly, with the publication of *Tierra Amarilla* in the United States, Ulibarrí reopens a path charted by Nuevomexicano writers centuries earlier. *Tierra Amarilla* thus becomes the link between "los de antes" whose goal was to document a disappearing way of life, and the harbingers of the Chicano generation of Nuevomexicano writers who openly fought against that disappearance.

The name—Tierra Amarilla—should evoke scenes of the armed conflict of 1967 that resulted when Reies López Tijerina led a small militia to take over the county courthouse and to reclaim the lost land grants of northern New Mexican families. The scenes evoked by Ulibarrí, however, are those of gilded childhood memories—a village nestled in a pastoral setting against a backdrop of the majestic Sangre de Cristo mountains. Against this backdrop, he spins yarns that depict an idyllic way of life as he nostalgically recalls it. Despite his picturesque vision there is a consciousness of something particular —a way of life that has since all but disappeared—which must be salvaged, recorded and demystified even as it is mystified. The entire collection is permeated with an impelling urge to recreate and preserve this vision. The picturesque tone of the first five short stories is balanced by a highly lyrical quality that reveals the poet Ulibarrí, and this tone is in turn counterbalanced by sharp wit and humor, which allow a glimpse of the *pícaro*[3] Ulibarrí. The polished dramatic style of the second half of the book demonstrates the breadth of Ulibarrí's craft. The last piece, a novella called "El hombre sin nombre," moves away from the *costumbrista*[4] vein to create a psychological study of the problem of self-identity and its relation to the creative process.

The story that opens the book, "Mi caballo mago," narrates the dreamlike experience of an adolescent protagonist/narrator in pursuit of an illusory horse. Implicit in the adventure is the symbolic pursuit of Manhood; as such, the story contains the elements of the *bildungsroman,* the narration of a coming-of-age adventure. The lyricism of this story sets it apart from the rest of the collection. A poem in prose, it has the quality of a fairy tale, of an interior journey into the fantasy world of the narrator.

The most striking element of "El caballo mago" is the swiftness with which we are drawn into the story's world. This is accomplished in the first paragraph by the rhythm of short, compact sentences, the repetition of the verb *era* (was) before descriptive adjectives, the parallel structure of the sentences, and rhyming patterns more characteristic of poetry than of prose:

> Era blanco. Blanco como el olvido. Era libre. Libre como la alegría. Era la ilusión, la libertad y la emoción. Poblaba y dominaba las serranías y las llanuras de las cercanías. Era un caballo blanco que llenó mi juventud de fantasía y poesía. (p. 3)
> (He was white. White as memories lost. He was free. Free as hapiness is. He was fantasy, liberty, and excitement. He filled and dominated the mountain valleys and surrounding plains. He was a white horse that flooded my youth with dreams and poetry.) (p. 2)

This elliptical style with full but staccato sentences continues throughout the story to create a feeling of suspense as events unfold rapidly in a manner reminiscent of dream imagery. By the time the narrator reveals himself as a fifteen-year-old protagonist, the readers already have abandoned themselves to the world of fantasy in which the white magic horse roams. But the phantom horse is not a dream; he is as real as the hired hands' campfire yarns that first introduce the young boy to this magnificent horse who will haunt his dreams and waking hours. Through the use of short paragraphs, a bare-bones sentence structure, and imagery that changes with a rapid kaleidoscopic effect, we accompany the protagonist in his pursuit of this "poema del mundo viril" (p. 3) (this poem of the world of men).

Finally the horse is captured and the ritual of coming of age fulfilled. There follows an encounter with the adolescent's reticent but proud father, who shakes his hand uttering a stark "esos son hombres" (p. 15) (That was a man's job). In his pursuit of the magic white horse the young boy seeks above all else to impress his father, who stands as the prototypical image of Manhood. In the end, however, when the young boy frees the magic horse, he cries; his tears are not tears of sorrow but tears of joy, which come from recognizing that El Mago is once again free to roam forever and to fill the fantasies of child and man with the transcendent power of idealism and illusion.

As an opening story "Mi caballo mago" has a threefold purpose: 1) it draws the reader rapidly into the creative psyche of the narrator; 2) it introduces the important son-emulating-the-father theme, a leitmotiv in the collection, which, in the novella, will unfold as a struggle for freedom from the law of the father; 3) it establishes Tierra Amarilla as the setting for the entire collection. Thus, in tandem with the novella, "Mi caballo mago" serves as a framing device to give structural unity to the collection. We are reminded throughout the collection that Tierra Amarilla is a very real place with very real people. And in fact it is. Tierra Amarilla, Ulibarrí's childhood home, is a Hispanic village in northern New Mexico. In Ulibarrí's narrative this very real place, however, has a unique character that allows the existence of magic white horses and nurtures the lyrical sensibilities of its young boys. As the title suggests, Tierra Amarilla and its inhabitants assume a central role in the remaining stories.

The next four stories are about people in the village of Tierra Amarilla and the protagonist's relations to them. These four tales

reveal echoes of Hispanic costumbrismo and a strong dose of picaresque humor. The anecdotal and humorous quality, the detailed exterior rather than psychological sketching of the characters, the references to the customs of *el pueblo,* all define the kinship of these narratives to the *cuadro de costumbre* and, more specifically, to the regional sketch. The fact that the short story owes its existence in part to the sketch of manners often makes it difficult to define precisely where one begins and the other ends. In the case of Ulibarrí's collection of stories, the kinship is indeed apparent. While his stories are moored in the detailed description of setting and the sometimes satirical treatment of types rather than full-fledged psychologically developed characters, there exists in his narratives a strong dramatic and emotional tendency that moves them in the direction of the short story. There is also the covert presence of the narrator's personal experience. The perspective throughout is from the first person, and the narrator's sentiments and personal involvement appear throughout the collection. Since the title of the book refers to the narratives as stories we will continue to refer to them as such, keeping in mind the close kinship they bear to the sketch of manners.

Whereas "Mi caballo mago" reveals Ulibarrí's talent for creating poetic imagery and evoking strong sensorial responses, the title of the second story, "El relleno de Dios," warns that we are in the realm of humor. The language in this story takes on the verbose quality of satire. Elaborate description more typical of the costumbrista mode also is used to bring to life the narrator's memory of the village priest and his impact upon his parishioners, particularly upon the life of the adolescent protagonist. The hysterical reaction of the parishioners to the

priest's distorted Spanish bears testimony to the collective picaresque nature of el pueblo. Students of folk behavior will recognize in this particular attitude a phenomenon that is part of all ethnic humor—encouraging the distortion of the native language for the purpose of eliciting laughter at the expense of the outsider. In fact, José Reyna tells us that "The jokes that are most popular among Chicanos in Texas are jokes which are based on misunderstanding of language."[5]

The editors of an anthology of Chicano literature have made the following observation regarding the topic of cultural humor. It bears some relation to "El relleno de Dios":

> The function of humor in a colonized situation is of prime importance for it allows the oppressed to strike back symbolically, to annihilate and vanquish the oppressor. Chicanos have an abundant repertoire of humor about gringos. As we assess and absorb our history, we must project these images, for the cultural weapon of humor, applied to the oppressor, exposes his vulnerability.[6]

While Father Benito's parishioners may not recognize him as their oppressor, they certainly recognize him as an outsider and use every available opportunity to capitalize on his linguistic vulnerability.

Once the stage is set with a description of Father Benito and his devastatingly humorous effect on his parish, the folk picarismo narrows down to be centered on the figure of the protagonist. Though the story does not conform to the traditional structure and the social intent of the picaresque tale—to deliver a scathing social critique—it does bring to mind episodes of classic picaresque works in which the picaroon develops a

complex pattern of deceptive behavior in order to satisfy his wants and needs.

"El relleno de Dios" begins and ends with a focus on the angelic priest who possesses the power to move his audience to hysteria. Gratuitously interpolated between the episodes concerning Father Benito are picaresque scenes that switch the focus to the narrator. There is not sufficient thematic continuity to fuse the episodes into an organic whole, yet artistic unity is achieved through a very consciously elaborated style that fluctuates from a free flowing descriptive narrative technique to the staccato rhythm of compact, catalogued verbal enumerations designed to heighten dramatic tension. Unity also is achieved through the manipulation of language to create the sort of satirical humor that forms the core of the Hispanic picaresque tradition.

A collection of regional cuadros would be incomplete without a detailed account of the village drunk. The story entitled "Juan P." begins, in true costumbrista style, with a detailed description of the age-old custom of building a mound and a woodpile for winter. This introduction serves as the setting for the raconté of the main story, which focuses on the circumstances surrounding the ill-fated destiny of a once charming young man, now known as Juan Pedo and his sisters "las perrodas." The young narrator is chopping wood when Juan P. rides by on a proud sorrel, the only remaining vestige of his once honorable position. Until this moment the young boy had assumed that the nickname was a result of Juan's weakness for drinking since *pedo* (fart) is a term often used in northern New Mexico for that condition. Given the tendency of Nuevomexicanos to transform words through the process of

metathesis, he links the sisters' nickname, *las perrodas* (*pedorras* in formal Spanish) to Juan's condition. However, on this occasion he senses for the first time a tragic note behind Juan's off-keyed song and he insists that Brígido, one of his father's *peones*, reveal to him how Juan and his sisters acquired the humiliating nicknames. It is Brígido's account, then, that the narrator remembers and shares with the reader; the narrative strategy of embedding in this story centers authority on one who "knows the real story" and reveals it to the narrator. What the young boy discovers is that the village people, by capitalizing on an unfortunate accident that befell one of the sisters at a village wake, are responsible for the injustice against Juan and his sisters.

As Brígido ends his tale the young boy reacts with indignation to the senseless behavior of the village people who condemned three beings to a life of shame and ignominy. He pretends that each log is one of those vile village creatures and he chops furiously, avenging the good name of Juan and his sisters. This final note of criticism, the personal note of empathy and the colorful descriptions of the village customs, give this story a more clearly defined costumbrista quality.

"Sábelo" follows the patterns developed in "El relleno de Dios" and "Juan P." in that it centers around a member of the village who stands out as one of the more interesting types in the narrator's memory, Don José Viejo, who is older than "el hambre." As in the previous stories, this story follows the costumbrista tendency through allusions to and descriptions of village customs. An episode focusing on the narrator's boyhood activities, which bear only a tangential relation to the main character's story, discloses a structural parallel to "El relleno de

Dios." The central episode, or the revelation of Don José's mysterious relationship to the honey bee, takes a twist that is so fantastic in nature that the reader wants to read it as a fairy tale. However the fact that its source is the *anciano* (old one) who experienced the events, adds weight to its reliability as "truth" rather than fairy tale.

The salient cultural value revealed in this story is the importance of the village elders. Chicano people have traditionally displayed a deep reverence and respect for older people, believing they possess wisdom accessible only through age and experience. One of the main functions of *viejitos* is that of storyteller; they are the transmitters of the folklore and oral history, and, as such, they perform the critical function of shaping the contours and values of the culture. Thus, this story is one with which many Nuevomexicano readers can identify. It takes us back to our own childhood when we too trembled in awe before the fantastic tales of los viejitos, knowing that we had been touched by a magic power that they alone possessed.

"La fragua sin fuego" involves a level of interiorization of the main character not present in the previous sketches and includes another slight divergence in which the narrator dwells upon his own infatuation with Edumenio's wife. The focus then returns to the main character and, as in the story called "Juan P.," there is a tragic turn of events as Edumenio and his young bride, who is rumored by idle tongues to be a "loose woman," are rejected by a cruel village code. Once again we see the young boy react with indignation at this unwarranted collective behavior, but now the personal involvement of the narrator becomes far more dramatic as he addresses an emotional apology to Edumenio and Henriqueta. The closing tone of this

story reveals as no other story except "El caballo mago," the young narrator's sensitive nature. In this story we see that despite Ulibarrí's nostalgic vision of Tierra Amarilla and its inhabitants, he does not lose sight of the negative of collective behavior displayed by the people of *su tierra.*

A drastic change in tone in the novella, *El hombre sin nombre,* could lead one to believe that the two parts of the book bear no relation save a common author. Though the emphasis in this narrative falls in a different direction, there is one thread that weaves together the lyrically accented "El caballo mago," the costumbrista short stories, and the dramatic novella, thus rendering the work cohesive. This thread is introduced in the first story, though in a subtle way. While the story seems to focus on the young boy and the magic white horse, the reader is conscious of the fact that the entire story—the relations of the characters, and the actions of the protagonist—are controlled by a pivotal figure: the father.

In the stories that follow, the reader becomes more and more aware of the patriarchal nature of the society described by Ulibarrí. The position of the narrator, his attitude toward the villagers—the father's peones—is that of the patriarch's son. There is throughout the entire collection a sense of noblesse oblige typical of nineteenth-century Peninsular and Latin American Romanticism as it nostalgically documented the passing of feudal vestiges and patriarchal society and the arrival of bourgeois capitalist society with its narrative mode of social realism. It is from his position of social privilege that the narrator in the stories remembers, describes, judges, even pities his subjects. But in the novella the patriarch's son must face the conflict between the unconscious desire to maintain that

privilege—made manifest in the image of the patriarch that haunts the son's psyche—and the reality of living in a modern world in which individual worth is measured through action rather than filiation.

In the first part of the collection we see the young boy growing up in Tierra Amarilla. His sense of self is derived from his cultural milieu, his position vis-à-vis his father, and his privilege ascribed by that relation. In *El hombre sin nombre* young Alejandro Turriaga—his name being revealed to us for the first time in the novella—returns to Tierra Amarilla after having ventured out of his familiar cultural setting and familial womb into the modern world. He has returned to Tierra Amarilla to celebrate the completion of a book he has written about his father; but he has also returned to find himself. Alejandro's homecoming turns into a nightmare as he realizes that his dead father is still alive within him. A dramatic struggle ensues between Turriaga Sr. and Jr. as Alejandro attempts to free himself from the law of the father, which he learned to revere and desire in another time, in another world. The pursuit of the ideal of manhood in the fixed likeness and image of the patriarch developed in the first story turns into a more complex search and revelation as the focus shifts gradually to the process and significance of the creative endeavor.

If we view the battle with his father's ghost as a manifestation of the broader struggle to integrate two disparate experiences—that of his cultural past and that of living in a modern post-patriarchal world—the inversion of the initials of Tierra Amarilla in the initials of the protagonist's name Alejandro Turriaga becomes significant. In an effort to integrate his mature identity, it is essential that he return to the seed of his origin. Thus,

Alejandro Turriaga replaces Tierra Amarilla as the central focus of the novella as he sets about to confront his past and to reconcile its loss with the reality of living in the modern world.

In the course of the narrative development, the question of the protagonist's identity vis-à-vis his past is superceded by the problem of the protagonist-turned-author's identity in relation to his created world. The writer is faced with the realization that to create characters is to create or perhaps to allow new selves to take form. As he shapes his aesthetic credo, the protagonist/writer affirsm that he views writing as an act of going out of oneself, of encountering other selves who are, in effect, the catalysts of the creative process: "Quizá algún día con otro, yo, como el Alex en el libro, caiga desmayado, y de ahí surga otra novela" (p. 167). (Perhaps some day another I, like the Alex in the book, may fall unconscious, and from that beginning may spring another novel.)

With this allusion to a novel within a novel through the intrusion of the voice of the implied author of *Tierra Amarilla*, Ulibarrí delves deeper into his interpretation of the creative process. Through the protagonist/author we witness the altered state of consciousness into which the creative act casts the writer. This state represents the writer's return to the archetypal origin, or to a state of preconscious chaos where the creative impulse originates. While the ordering of chaos or the emergence to a conscious, symbolic state should help the writer reach integration, he, in effect discovers that the opposite is the case. The writer experiences the creation of fictitious characters as an act of identity multiplication; his characters are autonomous yet they are an extension of the writer's psyche. The proverbial question "*Quién soy?*" (Who am I?) thus remains

unanswered: "Yo sigo con mi tormento de no saber quién soy . . ." (p. 167). (I continued with my own torture due to my ignorance of who I am. . . .) The act of writing reveals to the author (fictitious and implied) that identity is never naive or unidimensional; it is dynamic construct that is psychological and metaphysical as well as collective and material. He is those who came before him and he is a unique self; he is an individual and he is part of a remembered and a shared collective experience; he is the flesh that experiences reality and he is the mind that creates it; but he is above all what he makes of himself through language. If this last statement remains hidden in the dense psychological trappings of *El hombre sin nombre*, perhaps another of his texts will shed light on what writing means to Ulibarrí:

> In the beginning was the Word. And the Word was made flesh. It was so in the beginning, and it is so today. The language, the Word, carries with it the history, the culture, the traditions, the very life of a people, the flesh. Language is people. We cannot even conceive of a language without a people. The two are one and the same. To know one is to know the other. . . . As his language fades, the Hispano's identity with a history, with a tradition, with a culture, become more nebulous with each passing day.[7]

Ulibarrí's strong sense of self as artist and as member of his ethnic community together with his intense sense of place make his work essential to this series.

Erlinda Gonzales-Berry
University of New Mexico

NOTES

1. See table of contents and introduction to *Pasó por aquí: Critical Essays on the New Mexican Literary Tradition, 1542–1988*, Erlinda Gonzales-Berry. Albuquerque: University of New Mexico Press, 1989.

2. Francisco Lomelí has called the first decade of publication of works by Chicano writers the Chicano Boom. See: "Novel" in *A Decade of Chicano Literature (1970–1979): Critical Essays and Bibliography*, eds. Luis Leal, Fernando de Necochea, Francisco Lomelí, Roberto G. Trujillo. Santa Barbara: Editorial La Causa, 1982, pp. 29–38.

3. Here I use the term picaroon, and later picaresque, in a loose fashion rather than in the strict literary sense of the word. My intent is to point out a kind of roguish folk behavior reminiscent of the Hispanic literary picaroon. It is customary among Nuevomexicanos to call a person who leans toward mischievous behavior a *pícaro*. Later, the term is used in the literary sense.

4. *Costumbrismo* was a literary style developed in the eighteenth century in Spain and later emulated in Latin America. This style corresponds roughly to the English language Sketch of Manners.

5. José Reyna, "Chicano Folklore: Raza Humor in Texas," *De Colores*, 1:4 (1974): 59.

6. Antonia Castañeda Shular, Joseph Sommers and Tomás Ybarra-Frausto, *Literatura Chicana: Texto y contexto*. Englewood Cliffs: Princeton Hall, Inc., p. 124.

7. Sabine Ulibarrí, "Cultural Heritage of the Southwest." *We Are Chicanos*, ed., Philip Ortego. New York: Washington Square Press, 1973, p. 14.

CONTENTS

TABLA DE MATERIAS

TIERRA AMARILLA

MY WONDER HORSE

He was white. White as memories lost. He was free. Free as happiness is. He was fantasy, liberty, and excitement. He filled and dominated the mountain valleys and surrounding plains. He was a white horse that flooded my youth with dreams and poetry.

Around the campfires of the country and in the sunny patios of the town, the ranch hands talked about him with enthusiasm and admiration. But gradually their eyes would become hazy and blurred with dreaming. The lively talk would die down. All thoughts fixed on the vision evoked by the horse. Myth of the animal kingdom. Poem of the world of men.

White and mysterious, he paraded his harem through the summer forests with lordly rejoicing. Winter sent him to the plains

Mi caballo mago

Era blanco. Blanco como el olvido. Era libre. Libre como la alegría. Era la ilusión, la libertad y la emoción. Poblaba y dominaba las serranías y las llanuras de las cercanías. Era un caballo blanco que llenó mi juventud de fantasía y poesía.

Alrededor de las fogatas del campo y en las resolanas del pueblo los vaqueros de esas tierras hablaban de él con entusiasmo y admiración. Y la mirada se volvía turbia y borrosa de ensueño. La animada charla se apagaba. Todos atentos a la visión evocada. Mito del reino animal. Poema del mundo viril.

Blanco y arcano. Paseaba su harén por el bosque de verano en regocijo imperial. El invierno decretaba el llano y la ladera para sus hembras. Veraneaba como rey de oriente en su jardín silvestre.

and sheltered hillsides for the protection of his females. He spent the summer like an Oriental potentate in his woodland gardens. The winter he passed like an illustrious warrior celebrating a well-earned victory.

He was a legend. The stories told of the Wonder Horse were endless. Some true, others fabricated. So many traps, so many snares, so many searching parties, and all in vain. The horse always escaped, always mocked his pursuers, always rose above the control of man. Many a valiant cowboy swore to put his halter and his brand on the animal. But always he had to confess later that the mystic horse was more of a man than he.

I was fifteen years old. Although I had never seen the Wonder Horse, he filled my imagination and fired my ambition. I used to listen open-mouthed as my father and the ranch hands talked about the phantom horse who turned into mist and air and nothingness when he was trapped. I joined in the universal obsession—like the hope of winning the lottery—of putting my lasso on him some day, of capturing him and showing him off on Sunday afternoons when the girls of the town strolled through the streets.

It was high summer. The forests were fresh, green, and gay. The cattle moved slowly, fat and sleek in the August sun and shadow. Listless and drowsy in the lethargy of late afternoon, I was dozing on my horse. It was time to round up the herd and go back to the good bread of the cowboy camp. Already my comrades would be sitting around the campfire, playing the guitar, telling stories of past or present, or surrendering to the languor of the late afternoon. The sun was setting behind me in a riot of streaks and colors. Deep, harmonious silence.

I sit drowsily still, forgetting the cattle in the glade. Suddenly

Invernaba como guerrero ilustre que celebra la victoria ganada.

Era leyenda. Eran sin fin las historias que se contaban del caballo brujo. Unas verdad, otras invención. Tantas trampas, tantas redes, tantas expediciones. Todas venidas a menos. El caballo siempre se escapaba, siempre se burlaba, siempre se alzaba por encima del dominio de los hombres. ¡Cuánto valedor no juró ponerle su jáquima y su marca para confesar después que el brujo había sido más hombre que él!

Yo tenía quince años. Y sin haberlo visto nunca el brujo me llenaba ya la imaginación y la esperanza. Escuchaba embobado a mi padre y a sus vaqueros hablar del caballo fantasma que al atraparlo se volvía espuma y aire y nada. Participaba de la obsesión de todos, ambición de lotería, de algún día ponerle yo mi lazo, de hacerlo mío, y lucirlo los domingos por a la tarde cuando las muchachas salen a paseo por la calle.

Pleno el verano. Los bosques verdes, frescos y alegres. Las reses lentas, gordas y luminosas en la sombra y en el sol de agosto. Dormitaba yo en un caballo brioso, lánguido y sutil en el sopor del atardecer. Era hora ya de acercarse a la majada, al buen pan y al rancho del rodeo. Ya los compañeros estarían alrededor de la hoguera agitando la guitarra, contando cuentos del pasado o de hoy o entregándose al cansancio de la tarde. El sol se ponía ya, detrás de mí, en escándalos de rayo y color. Silencio orgánico y denso.

Sigo insensible a las reses al abra. De pronto el bosque se calla. El silencio enmudece. La tarde se detiene. La brisa deja de

the forest falls silent, a deafening quiet. The afternoon comes to a standstill. The breeze stops blowing, but it vibrates. The sun flares hotly. The planet, life, and time itself have stopped in an inexplicable way. For a moment, I don't understand what is happening.

Then my eyes focus. There he is! The Wonder Horse! At the end of the glade, on high ground surrounded by summer green. He is a statue. He is an engraving. Line and form and white stain on a green background. Pride, prestige, and art incarnate in animal flesh. A picture of burning beauty and virile freedom. An ideal, pure and invincible, rising from the eternal dreams of humanity. Even today my being thrills when I remember him.

A sharp neigh. A far-reaching challenge that soars on high, ripping the virginal fabric of the rosy clouds. Ears at the point. Eyes flashing. Tail waving active defiance. Hoofs glossy and destructive. Arrogant ruler of the countryside.

The moment is never ending, a momentary eternity. It no longer exists, but it will always live. . . . There must have been mares. I did not see them. The cattle went on their indifferent way. My horse followed them, and I came slowly back from the land of dreams to the world of toil. But life could no longer be what it was before.

That night under the stars I didn't sleep. I dreamed. How much I dreamed awake and how much I dreamed asleep, I do not know. I only know that a white horse occupied my dreams and filled them with vibrant sound, and light, and turmoil.

Summer passed and winter came. Green grass gave place to white snow. The herds descended from the mountains to the valleys and the hollows. And in the town they kept saying that the Wonder Horse was roaming through this or that secluded area. I

respirar, pero tiembla. El sol se excita. El planeta, la vida y el tiempo se han detenido de una manera inexplicable. Por un instante no sé lo que pasa.

Luego mis ojos aciertan. ¡Allí está! ¡El caballo mago! Al extremo del abra, en un promontorio, rodeado de verde. Hecho estatua, hecho estampa. Línea y forma y mancha blanca en fondo verde. Orgullo, fama y arte en carne animal. Cuadro de belleza encendida y libertad varonil. Ideal invicto y limpio de la eterna ilusión humana. Hoy palpito todo aún al recordarlo.

Silbido. Reto trascendental que sube y rompe la tela virginal de las nubes rojas. Orejas lanzas. Ojos rayos. Cola viva y ondulante, desafío movedizo. Pezuña tersa y destructiva. Arrogante majestad de los campos.

El momento es eterno. La eternidad momentanea. Ya no está, pero siempre estará. Debió de haber yeguas. Yo no las vi. Las reses siguen indiferentes. Mi caballo las sigue y yo vuelvo lentamente del mundo del sueño a la tierra del sudor. Pero ya la vida no volverá a ser lo que antes fue.

Aquella noche bajo las estrellas no dormí. Soñé. Cuánto soñé despierto y cuánto soñé dormido yo no sé. Sólo sé que un caballo blanco pobló mis sueños y los llenó de resonancia y de luz y de violencia.

Pasó el verano y entró el invierno. El verde pasto dió lugar a la blanca nieve. Las manadas bajaron de las sierras a los valles y cañadas. Y en el pueblo se comentaba que el brujo andaba por

inquired everywhere for his whereabouts. Every day he became for me more of an ideal, more of an idol, more of a mystery.

It was Sunday. The sun had barely risen above the snowy mountains. My breath was a white cloud. My horse was trembling with cold and fear like me. I left without going to mass. Without any breakfast. Without the usual bread and sardines in my saddle bags. I had slept badly, but had kept the vigil well. I was going in search of the white light that galloped through my dreams.

On leaving the town for the open country, the roads disappear. There are no tracks, human or animal. Only a silence, deep, white, and sparkling. My horse breaks trail with his chest and leaves an unending wake, an open rift, in the white sea. My trained, concentrated gaze covers the landscape from horizon to horizon, searching for the noble silhouette of the talismanic horse.

It must have been midday. I don't know. Time had lost its meaning. I found him! On a slope stained with sunlight. We saw one another at the same time. Together, we turned to stone. Motionless, absorbed, and panting, I gazed at his beauty, his pride, his nobility. As still as sculptured marble, he allowed himself to be admired.

A sudden, violent scream breaks the silence. A glove hurled into my face. A challenge and a mandate. Then something surprising happens. The horse that in summer takes his stand between any threat and his herd, swinging back and forth from left to right, now plunges into the snow. Stronger than they, he is breaking trail for his mares. They follow him. His flight is slow in order to conserve his strength.

I follow. Slowly. Quivering. Thinking about his intelligence. Admiring his courage. Understanding his courtesy. The afternoon advances. My horse is taking it easy.

este o aquel rincón. Yo indagaba por todas partes su paradero. Cada día se me hacía más ideal, más imagen, más misterio.

Domingo. Apenas rayaba el sol de la sierra nevada. Aliento vaporoso. Caballo tembloroso de frío y de ansias. Como yo. Salí sin ir a misa. Sin desayunarme siquiera. Sin pan y sardinas en las alforjas. Había dormido mal y velado bien. Iba en busca de la blanca luz que galopaba en mis sueños.

Al salir del pueblo al campo libre desaparecen los caminos. No hay rastro humano o animal. Silencio blanco, hondo y rutilante. Mi caballo corta el camino con el pecho y deja estela eterna, grieta abierta, en la mar cana. La mirada diestra y atenta puebla el paisaje hasta cada horizonte buscando el noble perfil del caballo místico.

Sería medio día. No sé. El tiempo había perdido su rigor. Di con él. En una ladera contaminada de sol. Nos vimos al mismo tiempo. Juntos nos hicimos piedra. Inmóvil, absorto y jadeante contemplé su belleza, su arrogancia, su nobleza. Esculpido en mármol, se dejó admirar.

Silbido violento que rompe el silencio. Guante arrojado a la cara. Desafío y decreto a la vez. Asombro nuevo. El caballo que en verano se coloca entre la amenaza y la manada, oscilando a distancia de diestra a siniestra, ahora se lanza a la nieve. Más fuerte que ellas, abre la vereda a las yeguas. Y ellas lo siguen. Su fuga es lenta para conservar sus fuerzas.

Sigo. Despacio. Palpitante. Pensando en su inteligencia. Admirando su valentía. Apreciando su cortesía. La tarde se alarga. Mi caballo cebado a sus anchas.

One by one the mares become weary. One by one, they drop out of the trail. Alone! He and I. My inner ferment bubbles to my lips. I speak to him. He listens and is quiet.

He still opens the way, and I follow in the path he leaves me. Behind us a long, deep trench crosses the white plain. My horse, which has eaten grain and good hay, is still strong. Undernourished as the Wonder Horse is, his strength is waning. But he keeps on because that is the way he is. He does not know how to surrender.

I now see black stains over his body. Sweat and the wet snow have revealed the black skin beneath the white hair. Snorting breath, turned to steam, tears the air. White spume above white snow. Sweat, spume, and steam. Uneasiness.

I felt like an executioner. But there was no turning back. The distance between us was growing relentlessly shorter. God and Nature watched indifferently.

I feel sure of myself at last. I untie the rope. I open the lasso and pull the reins tight. Every nerve, every muscle is tense. My heart is in my mouth. Spurs pressed against trembling flanks. The horse leaps. I whirl the rope and throw the obedient lasso.

A frenzy of fury and rage. Whirlpools of light and fans of transparent snow. A rope that whistles and burns the saddle tree. Smoking, fighting gloves. Eyes burning in their sockets. Mouth parched. Fevered forehead. The whole earth shakes and shudders. The long, white trench ends in a wide, white pool.

Deep, gasping quiet. The Wonder Horse is mine! Both still trembling, we look at one another squarely for a long time. Intelligent and realistic, he stops struggling and even takes a hesitant step toward me. I speak to him. As I talk, I approach him. At first, he flinches and recoils. Then he waits for me. The

Una a una las yeguas se van cansando. Una a una se van quedando a un lado. ¡Solos! El y yo. La agitación interna reboza a los labios. Le hablo. Me escucha y calla.

El abre el camino y yo sigo por la vereda que me deja. Detrás de nosotros una larga y honda zanja blanca que cruza la llanura. El caballo que ha comido grano y buen pasto sigue fuerte. A él, mal nutrido, se la han agotado las fuerzas. Pero sigue porque es él y porque no sabe ceder.

Encuentro negro y manchas negras por el cuerpo. La nieve y el sudor han revelado la piel negra bajo el pelo. Mecheros violentos de vapor rompen el aire. Espumparajos blancos sobre la blanca nieve. Sudor, espuma y vapor. Ansia.

Me sentí verdugo. Pero ya no había retorno. La distancia entre nosotros se acortaba implacablemente. Dios y la naturaleza indiferentes.

Me siento seguro. Desato el cabestro. Abro el lazo. Las riendas tirantes. Cada nervio, cada músculo alerta y el alma en la boca. Espuelas tensas en ijares temblorosos. Arranca el caballo. Remolineo el cabestro y lanzo el lazo obediente.

Vértigo de furia y rabia. Remolinos de luz y abanicos de transparente nieve. Cabestro que silba y quema en la teja de la silla. Guantes violentos que humean. Ojos ardientes en sus pozos. Boca seca. Frente caliente. Y el mundo se sacude y se estremece. Y se acaba la larga zanja blanca en un ancho charco blanco.

Sosiego jadeante y denso. El caballo mago es mío. Temblorosos ambos, nos miramos de hito en hito por un largo rato. Inteligente y realista, deja de forcejar y hasta toma un paso hacia mí. Yo le hablo. Hablándole me acerco. Primero recula. Luego me espera.

two horses greet one another in their own way. Finally, I succeed in stroking his mane. I tell him many things, and he seems to understand.

Ahead of me, along the trail already made, I drove him toward the town. Triumphant. Exultant. Childish laughter gathered in my throat. With my newfound manliness, I controlled it. I wanted to sing, but I fought down the desire. I wanted to shout, but I kept quiet. It was the ultimate in happiness. It was the pride of the male adolescent. I felt myself a conqueror.

Occasionally the Wonder Horse made a try for his liberty, snatching me abruptly from my thoughts. For a few moments, the struggle was renewed. Then we went on.

It was necessary to go through the town. There was no other way. The sun was setting. Icy streets and people on the porches. The Wonder Horse full of terror and panic for the first time. He ran and my well-shod horse stopped him. He slipped and fell on his side. I suffered for him. The indignity. The humiliation. Majesty degraded. I begged him not to struggle, to let himself be led. How it hurt me that other people should see him like that!

Finally we reached home.

"What shall I do with you, Mago? If I put you into the stable or the corral, you are sure to hurt yourself. Besides, it would be an insult. You aren't a slave. You aren't a servant. You aren't even an animal."

I decided to turn him loose in the fenced pasture. There, little by little, Mago would become accustomed to my friendship and my company. No animal had ever escaped from that pasture.

My father saw me coming and waited for me without a word. A smile played over his face, and a spark danced in his eyes. He watched me take the rope from Mago, and the two of us

Hasta que los dos caballos se saludan a la manera suya. Y por fin llego a alisarle la crin. Le digo muchas cosas, y parece que me entiende.

Por delante y por las huellas de antes lo dirigí hacia el pueblo. Triunfante. Exaltado. Una risa infantil me brotaba. Yo, varonil, la dominaba. Quería cantar y pronto me olvidaba. Quería gritar pero callaba. Era un manojo de alegría. Era el orgullo del hombre adolescente. Me sentí conquistador.

El Mago ensayaba la libertad una y otra vez, arrancándome de mis meditaciones abruptamente. Por unos instantes se armaba la lucha otra vez. Luego seguíamos.

Fue necesario pasar por el pueblo. No había remedio. Sol poniente. Calles de hielo y gente en los portales. El Mago lleno de terror y pánico por la primera vez. Huía y mi caballo herrado lo detenía. Se resbalaba y caía de costalazo. Yo lloré por él. La indignidad. La humillación. La alteza venida a menos. Le rogaba que no forcejara, que se dejara llevar. ¡Cómo me dolió que lo vieran así los otros!

Por fin llegamos a la casa. "¿Qué hacer contigo, Mago? Si te meto en el establo o en el corral, de seguro te haces daño. Además sería un insulto. No eres esclavo. No eres criado. Ni siquiera eres animal." Decidí soltarlo en el potrero. Allí podría el Mago irse acostumbrando poco a poco a mi amistad y compañía. De ese potrero no se había escapado nunca un animal.

Mi padre me vió llegar y me esperó sin hablar. En la cara le jugaba una sonrisa y en los ojos le bailaba una chispa. Me vió quitarle el cabestro al Mago y los dos lo vimos alejarse, pensativos.

thoughtfully observed him move away. My father clasped my hand a little more firmly than usual and said, "That was a man's job." That was all. Nothing more was needed. We understood one another very well. I was playing the role of a real man, but the childish laughter and shouting that bubbled up inside me almost destroyed the impression I wanted to create.

That night I slept little, and when I slept, I did not know that I was asleep. For dreaming is the same when one really dreams, asleep or awake. I was up at dawn. I had to go to see my Wonder Horse. As soon as it was light, I went out into the cold to look for him.

The pasture was large. It contained a grove of trees and a small gully. The Wonder Horse was not visible anywhere, but I was not worried. I walked slowly, my head full of the events of yesterday and my plans for the future. Suddenly I realized that I had walked a long way. I quicken my steps. I look apprehensively around me. I begin to be afraid. Without knowing it, I begin to run. Faster and faster.

He is not there. The Wonder Horse has escaped. I search every corner where he could be hidden. I follow his tracks. I see that during the night he walked incessantly, sniffing, searching for a way out. He did not find one. He made one for himself.

I followed the track that led straight to the fence. And I saw that the trail did not stop but continued on the other side. It was a barbed-wire fence. There was white hair on the wire. There was blood on the barbs. There were red stains on the snow and little red drops in the hoofprints on the other side of the fence.

I stopped there. I did not go any farther. The rays of the morning sun on my face. Eyes clouded and yet filled with light.

Me estrechó la mano un poco más fuerte que de ordinario y me dijo: "Esos son hombres." Nada más. Ni hacía falta. Nos entendíamos mi padre y yo muy bien. Yo hacía el papel de *muy hombre* pero aquella risa infantil y aquel grito que me andaban por dentro por poco estropean la impresión que yo quería dar.

Aquella noche casi no dormí y cuando dormí no supe que dormía. Pues el soñar es igual, cuando se sueña de veras, dormido o despierto. Al amanecer yo ya estaba de pie. Tenía que ir a ver al Mago. En cuanto aclaró salí al frío a buscarlo.

El potrero era grande. Tenía un bosque y una cañada. No se veía el Mago en ninguna parte pero yo me sentía seguro. Caminaba despacio, la cabeza toda llena de los acontecimientos de ayer y de los proyectos de mañana. De pronto me di cuenta que había andado mucho. Aprieto el paso. Miro aprensivo a todos lados Empieza a entrarme el miedo. Sin saber voy corriendo. Cada vez más rápido.

No está. El Mago se ha escapado. Recorro cada rincón donde pudiera haberse agazapado. Sigo la huella. Veo que durante toda la noche el Mago anduvo sin cesar buscando, olfateando, una salida. No la encontró. La inventó.

Seguí la huella que se dirigía directamente a la cerca. Y vi como el rastro no se detenía sino continuaba del otro lado. El alambre era de púa. Y había pelos blancos en el alambre. Había sangre en las púas. Había manchas rojas en la nieve y gotitas rojas en las huellas del otro lado de la cerca.

Allí me detuve. No fui más allá. Sol rayante en la cara. Ojos nublados y llenos de luz. Lágrimas infantiles en mejillas varoniles

Childish tears on the cheeks of a man. A cry stifled in my throat. Slow, silent sobs.

Standing there, I forgot myself and the world and time. I cannot explain it, but my sorrow was mixed with pleasure. I was weeping with happiness. No matter how much it hurt me, I was rejoicing over the flight and the freedom of the Wonder Horse, the dimensions of his indomitable spirit. Now he would always be fantasy, freedom, and excitement. The Wonder Horse was transcendent. He had enriched my life forever.

My father found me there. He came close without a word and laid his arm across my shoulders. We stood looking at the white trench with its flecks of red that led into the rising sun.

Grito hecho nudo en la garganta. Sollozos despaciosos y silenciosos.

Allí me quedé y me olvidé de mí y del mundo y del tiempo. No sé cómo estuvo, pero mi tristeza era gusto. Lloraba de alegría. Estaba celebrando, por mucho que me dolía, la fuga y la libertad del Mago, la transcendencia de ese espíritu indomable. Ahora seguiría siendo el ideal, la ilusión y la emoción. El Mago era un absoluto. A mí me había enriquecido la vida para siempre.

Allí me halló mi padre. Se acercó sin decir nada y me puso el brazo sobre el hombro. Nos quedamos mirando la zanja blanca con flecos de rojo que se dirigía al sol rayante.

THE STUFFING OF THE LORD

Father Benito almost saved my soul. Certainly he put me on the road to salvation, a feat which shocked and surprised my parents and elicited admiring exclamations from all the townsfolk. And wherever he may now be, Father Benito probably still regards me as saved.

The truth is that up to the age of twelve I had never shown the least interest in religion, much less any inclination to the priesthood or any other hood, priestly or otherwise. I had, in fact, given many indications of traveling in the opposite direction.

That is the way things were going when Father Benito came to Tierra Amarilla for the first time. Tierra Amarilla has never been the same since that day, nor have any of us who used to live there.

El relleno de dios

El padre Benito casi casi me salvó el alma. Por cierto me puso en el camino de la salvación, produciéndoles a mis padres una espantosa sorpresa y exclamaciones de admiración a toda la población. Y allá donde Dios lo tenga el padre Benito me tendrá todavía por salvado.

La verdad es que hasta la edad de doce años no había mostrado yo ni el menor olor de santidad ni mucho menos ninguna inclinación al sacerdocio o ningún otro docio, sácer o no. Al contrario, había dado muchas muestras de ir encaminado en opuesta dirección.

Así andaban las cosas cuando llegó el padre Benito a Tierra Amarilla por primera vez. Tierra Amarilla no ha sido la misma

The good father brought us light and life, tenderness and joy. He filled the town with talk and gaiety. He drew us to the Kingdom of Heaven by the strangest method ever used in the history of religion. If dying of laughter is a good thing, Father Benito brought us to a good death many, many times.

He had a round, bald head like a pale pumpkin. In the center of the tremendous hood of the Franciscan habit, it seemed to be loose, placed there without reason. Its position looked so precarious that one expected to see it roll from its place at any moment. On his saintly, round, slightly foolish face there was always a fixed smile—a truly beatific expression. He wore rimless glasses, out of style even then, on the end of his nose. I don't know why. Certainly it was not for seeing. Perhaps they were the transparent vestments for an extremely naked face. It was a nudity, stemming from innocence, turned virtue and purity. His small paunch, round as the loaves of San Roque, was supported by a white cord. Biblical sandals completed the angelic image of the priest who filled the entire valley of Tierra Amarilla with affection and harmony.

He was like the sun. When he passed along the street, he scattered smiles and good humor about him, banishing shadows, warming the dying, animating the conversation, provoking an occasional burst of laughter. Mirth was his constant companion.

He spoke terrible Spanish, fluent but mutilated. He could not pronounce the word *reino* in his favorite expression, *el reino de Dios* (the Kingdom of God), but he repeated it so often that it acquired a strange, fatal importance. Saying mass, he used to chant in magisterial tones, "In order to enter into the *relleno* of God. . . ." *Relleno,* dear readers, sounds a little like *reino,* but it means "stuffing"! While the words and the ascending intonation

desde ese día, ni lo hemos sido nadie de los que allí vivíamos. Vino a traernos luz y vida, ternura y alegría. Vino a llenar el pueblo de conversación y de buen humor. A ganarnos para el reino de Dios de la manera más extraña en la historia de la religión. Si morirse de la risa es bueno, el padre Benito nos llevó al buen morir muchas veces.

Tenía la cabeza pequeña y desnuda, como una calabaza rubia. En el centro del tremendo cuello de la sotana franciscana parecía estar suelta, arbitrariamente colocada. Se veía allí tan precaria que se esperaba que a cualquier momento rodara de su lugar. En su cara buena y redonda, un poco lela, vivía fija una sonrisa—una expresión verdaderamente beatífica—. Sobre la punta de la nariz llevaba unos espejuelos, fuera de moda aun entonces, no sé con qué motivo. Seguramente no eran para ver. Tal vez serían el transparente vestuario de una cara ya excesivamente desnuda—una desnudez hacia la inocencia, hecha virtud y pureza—. Una barriga global y diminuta, como el pan de San Roque, sostenida por una soga blanca, y unas sandalias bíblicas completaban la estampa angelical del sacerdote que llenó de amor y simpatías todo el valle de Tierra Amarilla.

Era como el sol. Cuando pasaba por la calle iba repartiendo por todos lados sonrisas y buen humor, eliminando sombras, calentando a los moribundos, animando la conversación, provocando una que otra carcajada. Sembraba vida dondequiera que iba. La risa era su compañera.

Hablaba un castellano espantoso, feliz y bárbaro. No podía pronunciar la palabra *reino*, y era su palabra predilecta. La empleaba tanto que el vocablo adquiría más trascendencia que de ordinario. Cuando entonaba en la misa cantada en tono magistral: "Para entrar en el relleno de Dios . . ." Las palabras y la

seemed to build a stairway to heavenly places, the faithful were in misery. They were broken up. They squirmed, they hunched their shoulders and lowered their heads. Spasms. Contortions. Agony. Fierce and fatal laughter, unbearable because it had to be contained.

The Father's ignorance of the language forced him to inquire about words when he was preparing his sermons. On one occasion, he asked a waggish character the word for "foundation," since he planned to preach a sermon about the poor condition of the substructure of the church.

Nobody ever stayed away from mass while Father Benito was in Tierra Amarilla. As usual, the church was full. The good priest began to scold us with his usual sincerity and fervor.

"You neglect your church. You are a disgrace to your religion. Today, there will be a special collection to provide fundaments for this church. The fundaments we have now are filthy, they have a bad odor. . . ." Nobody heard another word.

I doubt that in the history of Catholicism any priest ever had as unusual and eccentric an audience as Father Benito—without his ever knowing it. It was a congregation of convulsed faces, puffed cheeks, trembling chins, and bulging eyes. Noses were blown. Arms and legs twitched. Ears turned purple. Groans, moans, stifled cries—strange noises. The parishioners lowered their heads, bit their lips, held their stomachs, shuddered and shook. They were in agony.

The saintly priest from his pulpit, blind and deaf to what was going on, looked over his glasses at the bowed heads of the faithful. He saw them overcome by religious fervor. Virtuous and sincere, he gave us his best, he became more and more eloquent, he soared to the heights of passionate feeling.

entonación escalonadas como si de veras nos construyera una escalera a la zona celestial, los fieles se petrificaban, se deshacían, se estiraban, se encogían, se morían. Espasmos. Contorsiones. Agonías. Risa feroz y fatal. Risa contenida. Risa escondida.

Como no conocía bien la lengua preguntaba para preparar sus sermones. En una ocasión le preguntó a un sirvengüenza cómo se decía *foundation* porque esperaba hacer un sermón con motivos de las tristes condiciones de los cimientos de la iglesia.

Nadie faltaba a misa mientras el padre Benito fue sacerdote de Tierra Amarilla. Esta vez la iglesia estaba llena. El buen cura con su acostumbrada sinceridad y pasión, nos empezó a reñir: "Vosotros no tenéis vergüenza. Hoy habrá una colecta especial para ponerle fundillo a la iglesia. El fundillo de la iglesia está podrido, huele mal . . ." De seguro nadie pudo oír más.

No creo que haya habido en la historia del Catolicismo un cura que haya tenido un auditorio tan extraordinario, tan estrambótico, como el padre Benito—sin que él se diera cuenta nunca—. La de caras convulsionadas, mejillas sopladas, barbas temblorosas, ojos saltados, narices infladas, brazos y piernas agónicos, orejas moradas. Gemidos, lamentos, gritos, chasquidos, ruidos raros. Todos bajaban la cabeza, se mordían el labio, se apretaban el estómago, se estremecían, se sacudían. Se morían.

El santo cura, desde su púlpito, ciego y sordo, miraba sobre sus gafas a los fieles con la cabeza baja, consumidos por el fervor religioso. Virtuoso y sincero se esmeraba cada vez más, se volvía más y más elocuente, se remontaba a las esferas de su propia pasión.

All of us left the church exhausted. Pale, spent, with tears still in our eyes. We went home in silence. Without speaking. Without laughing. Without strength for anything else. Later, some other day, we would laugh. Then we would talk it over. Not now. Suppressed laughter is a savage beast in a cage.

Of course, nobody talked about anything else. The acolytes talked, too. They said that our beloved priest had one other peculiarity that they alone knew about. He did not like wine! The nuns always filled the little jar for communion, and he left it almost full. I had heard my father and other men say that priests had the best wine in the world. For that reason and no other, I entered on the path of salvation.

For the first time, I began to pay attention at catechism. I stopped asking the impertinent questions that had brought me so many catholic, apostolic, and Roman lumps on the head. I learned to lower my eyes properly and humbly at the least pretext and also to roll them piously upward toward the electric light bulb among the cracks and spider webs of the ceiling. I answered the questions of the priests and the nuns correctly, without creating the least disturbance. In short, I became so extremely sanctimonious that I surpassed the oldest and ugliest female fanatics of the area.

My parents did not know about all this, since it happened at school. Occasionally, an aunt or a friend would remark to my mother that I was behaving myself very well and that it was high time. Once when this happened in my presence, my mother looked at me suspiciously. The conversation continued, however, and she forgot about it. I never knew whether my father found out.

But in the convent school, the word certainly got around. The happiness of the sisters was almost more than they could bear. It was a miracle. I had been a student of theirs for six years, and

Salíamos todos molidos. Pálidos, agotados, las lágrimas todavía en los ojos. En silencio nos íbamos a casa. Sin hablar. Sin reír. Sin fuerzas para más. Más tarde, otro día, nos reiríamos. Entonces hablaríamos. Ahora no. La risa atada es una fiera encerrada.

Claro que no se hablaba de otra cosa. Los monaguillos también hablaban. Decían que el querido cura tenía una singularidad más, que sólo ellos conocían. ¡Al buen cura no le gustaba el vino! Las monjas le llenaban un jarrito de vino para la comunión y lo dejaba casi lleno. Yo había oído decir a mi padre y a otros que los curas tenían el mejor vino del mundo. Por eso, y no por otra cosa, entré yo en el camino de la salvación.

Empecé, por primera vez, a poner atención en el catecismo. Dejé de hacer las preguntas bochornosas que antes habían ganado tantos coscorrones católicos, apostólicos y romanos. Aprendí a bajar los ojos debida y humildemente a cualquier pretexto, y también a volverlos en blanco, elevándolos piadosamente hacia la bombilla eléctrica entre las rendijas y telarañas del cielo. Contestaba correctamente a las preguntas del cura y de las monjas sin hacer el menor escándalo. En fin, llegué a tal extremo de beatería (rima con bellaquería) que resulté más beato (rima con bellaco) que la más fea y más vieja de las beatas de mi tierra.

Como todo esto ocurría en la escuela, mis padres no supieron. Una que otra vez una tía o una amiga le observaba a mi madre que yo me estaba portando muy bien en la escuela y que ya era tiempo. Una vez que esto ocurrió en mi presencia mi madre me miró descreída y sospechosa, pero como la conversación continuó, se olvidó de ello. Si mi padre supo algo yo no lo supe.

Pero en el convento sí se sonó. Las monjas no daban con las que perdían de alegría. Era un milagro. Yo había sido su alumno por seis años, y esos seis años habían sido un pulgatorio. (Así

those six years had been purgatory for them—and for me, too. For a long time, I carried a body full of welts as holy testimony to my suffering.

No one can possibly know the joy—I mean delirium—I should say ecstasy—of a devoted sister who carries an unregenerate, submissive sinner and lays him in the lap of the Lord. I saw their rhapsodic glances and trembled, but not with pleasure. There is something frenzied and frightening about a woman in ecstasy. When I saw them, my hair stood on end, or, as one could say, reached toward heaven. The latter seemed to be their interpretation.

They became gentle, sweet, and kindly toward me. In my new role of lamb, or little suckling pig, I accepted their kindnesses. The most generous of all was Sister Generosa.

The nuns had charge of the altar and of dressing the saints. One day, when I felt that my campaign had achieved its purpose, I presented myself to be dressed—as an altar boy, of course. That day, there was rejoicing in the fields of the Lord, at least in one of them.

Thus began my religious career. It soon became evident that there was great promise in the new acolyte. During the *Mea culpa*, my chest pounding resounded throughout the tiny temple. My *amens* were the most amenable that had ever been heard in that region. All the way to the *Ite Missa est*, I was the most attentive and zealous of the crowd.

There were two altar boys. Completely organized. The priest fawned upon by the good ladies of the town. The sisters lining up the children. We tidying up, folding, arranging, in the sacristy. One swallow for me. One for you. Another for me. First we drank the wine and then we sniffed the jar dry. When Sister Generosa

dicen en mi tierra, y acaso tienen razón), para ellas y también para mí. Yo llevé por mucho tiempo un millón de ronchas en santo testimonio de esa penitencia.

Ustedes no pueden saber el placer, digo delirio, digo éxtasis de una buena religiosa que lleva a un pecador entero y sumiso y lo pone en el regazo del Señor. Yo miraba sus miradas rapsódicas y me estremecía, y no de placer. Hay algo furibundo y espantoso en la mujer extasiada. Cuando yo las veía se me ponían los pelos en punta, como quien dice, alzados también al cielo. Así parecía que lo interpretaban ellas.

Se pusieron tan blandas, tan dulces, tan generosas conmigo. Yo hecho corderito, lechoncito, me dejaba hacer. La más generosa de todas era la hermana Generosa.

Las monjas se encargaban del altar y de vestir a los santos. Un día, cuando ya creí que mi campaña debía haber logrado su fin, me presenté a que me vistieran a mí—de monaguillo, claro—. Ese día hubo regocijo y alegría en los campos del Señor, por lo menos en uno.

Así empezó mi carrera religiosa. Pronto se hizo patente que había gran promesa en el nuevo acólito. Durante el *Mea culpa* mis golpes de pecho resonaban por todo el minúsculo templo. Mis *Amenes* eran los más amenos que jamás se habían oído en aquel recinto. Y cuando venía el *Ite Missa est*, yo era el más atento y el más ferviente de la concurrencia.

Eramos dos. Todo organizado. El cura embaucado con las buenas señoras del pueblo. Las monjas desfilando a los niños. Nosotros alzando, doblando, limpiando. Un trago para mí. Uno para tí. Otro para mí. Primero nos bebíamos el vino y después aspirábamos lo que quedaba. Cuando entraba la hermana

came in, the heavenly jar was empty, completely clean. Neither she nor any of the sisters ever knew that Father Benito did not like wine.

I accompanied Father Benito to many a wedding and many a funeral. He with his hyssop and I with the censer. The odor of sanctity must be something like the smell of that smoke. At all these festivities, they served the priest first from the best they had, then his assistant, naturally. For the intelligent assistant, there is a good swig behind each blessing and a blessing in each swig. I always returned from these expeditions spiritually enriched. That life was becoming more and more fascinating to me.

My mother always accompanied me to high mass, the one read by Father Benito. I was now beginning to give her something to be proud of, whereas formerly I had given her only trouble. At least that is what I thought, although I frequently suspected that she was not really convinced of my conversion. But at any rate, the women of the town who used to have so many complaints about me, now heaped me with praises. It was a well-deserved rest for my mother.

My father never saw me or heard me at the altar, except for my baptism and first communion. Due to a series of unexpected incidents, he had to go on trips most weekends when I was displaying my chest-beating and my amenable amens. Some Sundays he had to go to six o'clock mass because of pressing duties. And unfortunately he contracted a mysterious illness which struck him on five successive Sundays and prevented his attending mass. His friends were much concerned, for they said he had not been seen for months. This troubled me a great deal. How I wanted to impress him—for the first time! Wasn't I now a real personality?

Generosa ya el jarro divino estaba vacío, seco y limpio. Ella, ninguna de ellas, nunca supo que al padre Benito no le gustaba el vino.

Acompañé al padre Benito a tanta boda y a tanto funeral. El con su hisopo, yo con la ollita de humo. El olor de santidad debe ser como el de ese humo. En todas estas fiestas al cura le sirven primero y de lo mejor, y a su ayudante, naturalmente. Para el ayudante inteligente hay un buen lamparillazo detrás de cada bendición y una bendición en cada lamparillazo. Yo siempre volvía de esas expediciones espiritualmente enriquecido. Esa vida me estaba cautivando cada vez más.

Mi madre me acompañaba siempre a la misa mayor, la del padre Benito. Ya yo empezaba a darle cartel donde antes le había dado mārtirio. Por lo menos eso creía yo, aunque con frecuencia tenía la sospecha de que ella no estaba nada convencida de mi conversión. El hecho es que las señoras del pueblo que antes sólo tenían quejas de mí ahora la colmaban de alabanzas. Era un descanso bien merecido.

Mi padre nunca me vio ni me oyó en el altar, excepto para mi bautismo y mi primera comunión. Por una serie de accidentes tuvo que emprender viaje la mayor parte de los fines de semana de mis sonoros golpes de pecho y mis *amenes* amenos. Algunos domingos tuvo que asistir a la misa de las seis por obligaciones imprescindibles. Y desgraciadamente tuvo una enfermedad misteriosa que le dio repentinamente cinco domingos seguidos que no le permitió asistir a misa. Sus amigos andaban muy alarmados porque decían que no se había dejado ver por meses. A mí me molestó esto mucho. ¡Cómo habría querido impresionarlo de veras —y por la primera vez! ¿No era yo ya personaje?

The usual thing happened to us. They took our good Father Benito away from us. I did not know what to do. My whole new life was abruptly ended. We said goodbye. I with deeply sincere tears. He with a sad smile. There are priests who inspire heartfelt love, others who are loved from a sense of duty, and, one must confess, some who are never loved at all. Father Benito belonged to the first group.

The day he left, the whole town came out to bid him goodbye. I do not think there was a dry eye in the crowd. That innocent spirit went away without knowing what he had brought us, without knowing what had happened. Without knowing what he was taking away with him. He carried with him much of the day's brightness, much laughter, and much happiness. He left us only the knowledge that we would never again know the same measure of those qualities. I believe that I felt his departure more than anyone else.

I returned to my post the next Sunday with the new priest. It was not the same. My chest pounding sounded dull and hollow. My amens lacked the old resonance. When the moment of communion arrived, I poured the accustomed amount of the sacramental wine. The priest shook the divine vessel impatiently. Reluctantly, I poured a little more. He insisted. Finally, I poured it all.

How indecent that seemed to me! What bad taste! I was—well, not raging, because that would have been a sacrilege at the altar—but something very much like it until the *Ite Missa est,* which rang down the final curtain on my religious career.

I returned to my old ways and my old pranks. I acted almost as I had before, almost but not quite. Something new, something unforeseen, had come to me in Father Benito's wine. I could not forget the good priest. My parents were surprised once more, but I think they were relieved and secretly thanked God. One thing is

Como ocurre con tanta frecuencia, a los buenos curas siempre se los llevan. Nos quitaron a nuestro buen padre Benito. Yo no sabía qué hacer. Toda una vida abruptamente terminada. Nos despedimos. Yo con lágrimas muy sinceras. El con una sonrisa triste.

Hay curas que se quieren de corazón, otros que se quieren de obligación, y fuerza es decirlo, hay otros que no se quieren de ninguna manera. El padre Benito fue de los primeros.

El día que el padre Benito se fue todo el pueblo salió a despedirlo. No creo que hubiera ojos secos. Se fue aquel hombre puro sin saber lo que había traído, sin saber lo que había pasado. Sin saber lo que se llevaba. Se llevó mucha de la luz del día, tanta risa y tanta alegría. Nos dejó la conciencia de que no volveríamos nunca a conocer la alegría, la risa y la luz en la misma medida. Yo creo haber sentido su partida más que nadie.

Volví el primer domingo con el nuevo cura. Ya no era igual. Mis golpes de pecho, sordos, huecos. Mis *Amenes* sin resonancia. Cuando llegó el momento de la comunión, yo le eché el pisto de costumbre. El cura me sacudió el divino vaso de oro impaciente. Le echo un poco más, resistiéndome. El insiste. Se lo echo todo. ¡Qué indecente me pareció aquello, qué mal gusto! Estuve, no rabiando, porque eso sería sacrílego en el altar, pero algo parecido hasta el *Ite Missa est* que fue el telón final de mi carrera religiosa.

Volví a mis fechorías y a mis andanzas. Hice mis cosas otra vez como antes, pero no del todo como antes. Algo me había ocurrido entretanto. Algo me vino con el vino. Al buen cura no lo pude olvidar. Mis padres se sorprendieron otra vez, pero creo que se aliviaron y dieron gracias a Dios en secreto. Lo cierto es que mi padre no tuvo ya que salir de viaje los domingos y que su misterioso mal desapareció. Volvimos a asistir a misa como

sure—my father no longer had to go away on Sundays and his mysterious illness disappeared. Once again we went to mass as a family. My mother between us giving a pinch to my father and another to me in moments when they were needed.

The years passed. My parents had died by this time. My siblings and I were now living in Santa Fe. We saw in the newspaper that a friend of ours, Flavio Hernández, had died. The rosary would be in the Salazar Funeral Home, and Father Benito would conduct the service!

I don't know which of our two motives was more powerful. We wanted to pay our respects to the dead, but we were also very eager to see Father Benito again. When we reached the mortuary, which was unfamiliar to us, we followed some people who were entering and found ourselves in a chapel where the deceased lay.

My sister, my brother, and I entered respectfully, our heads bowed. We threaded our way through the crowd, approached the coffin, knelt and began to pray. I tried to think about my prayers, but my thoughts kept going back to Tierra Amarilla and Father Benito. I remembered that at that time I had a very vague idea of what the Kingdom of God might be, but that I had a very clear and grotesque image of what the *relleno de Dios* might be. The revival of that memory started in me the silent tickling of a mad mirth. There is no laughter so wicked as that which strikes in a serious or sacred place.

I was trying to control myself when my brother nudged me. I heard a frightened whisper, "That isn't Flavio!" I raise my eyes and look. Not only is it not Flavio, but is a woman! I nudge my sister. She looks. We all stare. We turn our heads. We are surrounded by people we don't know.

Suddenly, without any warning, wild laughter swirls inside us.

familia otra vez. Mi madre entre nosotros con un pellizco para mi padre y otro para mí en los momentos oportunos.

Pasaron los años. Mis padres habían muerto ya. Vivíamos, mis hermanos y yo, en Santa Fe ahora. Vimos en el periódico que había muerto un amigo nuestro, Flavio Hernández, que el rosario tendría lugar en la casa mortuoria de Salazar —y que el padre Benito rezaría el rosario.

No sé cual de los motivos tendría mas influencia. Queríamos visitar al difunto, pero también teníamos muchas ansias de volver a ver al padre Benito. Cuando llegamos a la mortuoria, desconocida para nosotros, seguimos a unas personas que iban entrando y nos hallamos en la capilla donde estaba tendido el difunto.

Entramos mi hermana, mi hermano y yo, respetuosamente, con la cabeza baja. Pasamos por entre la gente, nos acercamos al cuerpo y nos pusimos de rodillas y empezamos a rezar. Yo trataba de pensar en mis oraciones pero mis pensamientos se me iban a Tierra Amarilla y al padre Benito. Recordaba que entonces tenía yo muy vaga noción de lo que fuera el reino de Dios pero que sí tenía una imagen muy clara y muy grotesca de lo que podría ser el *relleno* de Dios. Al despertar el recuerdo empecé a sentir el cosquilleo silencioso de una risa loca. No hay risa tan atrevida como la que nace en sitio serio o sagrado.

En estas cavilaciones estaba cuando me pica mi hermano con el codo y me dice al oído, como asustado, "¡No es Flavio!" Alzo los ojos y miro. ¡No sólo no es Flavio, sino que es una mujer! Le pico a mi hermana. Mira. Nos miramos. Volvemos la cara. Estamos rodeados de gente desconocida.

De pronto, sin anuncio ninguno, nos retoza la risa. Lo absurdo

The absurdity of that situation is too much. We do everything possible to control ourselves, but to no avail. We bite our lips. Our abdomens ache. Our faces become livid, congested. The suffering is indescribable. One of the others breaks out in a snort. We have to hide this, cover it up. I begin to weep noisily. My brother and sister follow my lead. Our tears flow freely. Our cries become more and more despairing. Hastily we stumble out, blind with tears and suffering. The real mourners have nothing to complain about. Our lamentations were certainly the hit of the year and the pride of the mortuary.

We reached home exhausted, literally sick. We should laugh and talk about it another day, but now it was impossible, as in the days of Father Benito and his masses. That night Father Benito made us laugh as he had in the old days. Without even seeing him. His physical presence was not needed. His trademark is laughter.

Always, when someone laughs deeply and helplessly, I think about the good father and laugh, too. And wonder how many souls may have reached heaven, having died laughing, saved that way by Saint Benito. I don't know what has become of him, but I am sure that he is still living. Certainly the day he enters the *relleno de Dios,* we will hear the peals of laughter, the cries, the guffaws, and the moans of the saints and the little angels—all this followed by long silences.

de aquello se apodera de nosotros. Hacemos lo posible por dominarnos. No hay remedio. Nos mordemos el labio. Nos duele el estómago. La cara lívida, congestionada. El sufrimento es indecible. Alguien revienta. Hay que ocultar, disimular. Suelto el llanto. Mis hermanos me acompañan. Las lágrimas corren libres. Los gritos cada vez más desesperados. Salimos corriendo, histéricos, ciegos de lágrimas y de dolor. Los verdaderos dolientes no tienen por qué quejarse. La lamentación nuestra seguramente fue el éxito del año y de la mortuoria.

Llegamos a casa exhaustos, enfermos, para reír y comentar otro día, porque ahora no se podía, como en aquellos días del padre Benito y de sus misas. Esa noche el padre Benito nos hizo reír como antes lo hiciera. Sin verlo siquiera. No hizo falta su presencia. Su divisa es la risa.

Siempre, cuando alguien se ríe de veras, pienso en él y me sonrío o me río. Y me pregunto cuántos no habrán llegado al cielo muertos de la risa, salvados por este San Benito. No sé qué ha sido de él pero estoy seguro que no ha muerto todavía. Por cierto el día que entre en el relleno de Dios oiremos todas las risotadas y carcajadas, los gemidos y los gritos de los santos y de los angelitos —todo esto seguido por largos silencios.

THE FRATER FAMILY

A stranger must be mystified by the rounded hummocks, evidently artificial, that stand close to all the houses in Tierra Amarilla. Especially in summer, when these mounds are bare, they look out of place, with no reason for existing.

In winter, however, stacks of firewood rise upon them like small cathedrals. The logs, entire trunks of trees, are stood on end and leaned against one another, more or less perpendicularly, to facilitate moving them one by one as they are needed. This way of stacking wood also provides the best ventilation in times of rain or snow.

The first thing that is swept after every snowfall is this hillock and the wood pile. Since it is always in a sunny spot and since the

Juan P.

Al forastero deben mistificarle unos montones, evidentemente artificiales, que hay en Tierra Amarilla al lado y muy cerca de todas las casas. Esto especialmente en el verano, porque entonces se ven mondos e incongruos sin aparente razón de ser.

En el invierno se ven allí, sobre los montones, rimeros de leña que se alzan como pequeñas catedrales. Se ponen los leños, troncos enteros de árboles secos, de punta, más o menos perpendiculares y arrimados unos a los otros, para facilitar su adquisición, uno por uno, conforme se van necesitando. Esta manera de apilar la leña proporciona también la mayor ventilación para la leña cuando viene la lluvia y la nieve.

Después de cada nevada lo primero que se barre es este

logs are on a slant, the water soon drains off and they dry out. In cold country, firewood has to be dry.

New houses have no mounds beside them. The wood pile is on level ground. But wood is chopped there day after day, year after year, generation after generation. Splinters, bark, and sawdust keep accumulating, growing, forming the dome which now adorns every homestead. One can almost deduce the age and economic status of the families by the height and width of the mound on the property.

My father was obsessed by the idea that I was now grown up. A country man, strong and robust, he was troubled by my predilection for books, especially for poetry. He had set up a schedule of tasks that left neither time nor energy for the least digression. This infuriated me, as I remember, especially since there were servants (we called them "hired hands") who could very well do these things. No, I could not appreciate this treatment at the time, though now I am grateful for it. One of my tasks was to cut the firewood. This was no small matter for a big house like ours. The problem looms even larger when you consider that I was attending school and that winter afternoons are not very long.

One Saturday, when the deep snow sparkled under a bright sun, I was cutting wood. Sitting on a log watching me was Brígido, one of the hired hands who had finished his work and was enjoying the sun and his cigarette. I think, too, that he was glorying in seeing me humiliated that way. Although I often hated him, the truth is that we were friends. From time to time, to rest or just to chat, I leaned on the axe handle and we talked. Brígido knew a lot, it seemed to me, and he used to tell me things that were real

promontorio y la pila de leña. Como siempre está en la resolana, y como tiene soslayo, pronto se escurre y pronto se seca. En tierras frías la leña tiene que estar seca.

Las casas nuevas no tienen montón. La pila de leña está en el plano. Pero allí se parte leña día tras día año por año, generación tras generación. Las briznas, las cortezas y el aserrín se van acumulando, creciendo, formando la cúpula que hoy adorna cada propiedad. Casi se puede deducir la edad y cualidad de las familias por la altura y la anchura del dombo del solar.

Mi padre tenía la manía de que yo fuera hombre. Hombre de campo, robusto y fuerte, le molestaba mi predilección por los libros, especialmente por la poesía. Me había decretado un régimen de quehaceres que no dejaban tiempo ni alientos para la menor divagación. Esto me envenenaba la sangre de una manera violenta, según recuerdo, especialmente cuando había criados (peones como les decíamos) que bien podían hacerlo. No, no supe apreciarlo entonces, aunque ahora se lo agradezco mucho.

Una de esas tareas era partir la leña. Para una casa grande, como la nuestra, eso no era poco. Esto tiene mayor significación si se considera que yo asistía a la escuela y que en invierno las tardes no son largas.

Un sábado de mucha nieve y mucho sol estaba yo partiendo leña. Sentado en un tronco cuidándome trabajar estaba Brígido, uno de los peones que había terminado su labor y se deleitaba con el sol y su cigarro. Creo, además, que se jactaba en verme así reducido. Aunque yo lo odiara con frecuencia, en verdad éramos amigos. De vez en cuando, para descansar o simplemente por conversar, me apoyaba en el cabo del hacha y hablábamos. Brígido sabía mucho, me parecía entonces, y me decía cosas que para un

revelations to a fifteen-year-old boy, things about women and witchcraft and love.

That is what we were doing when we saw a rider approaching. We soon recognized him. It was John F. John had a magnificent sorrel horse. It was his pride and the envy of everyone else. Tall, spirited, elegant, and as fat and shiny as a china cup. There wasn't a sport in the whole county who didn't want to buy it or trade him for it. But John always refused with a smile of internal satisfaction and a faint touch of scorn, although he could well have used the money which was badly needed at his house.

John was riding along singing. He always sang when he was drunk. Today was no exception. The strange thing was what he was singing. At first we could not distinguish the words. The only thing noticeable was how nasal and petulant his voice was and, of course, how much off-key. Finally we heard the song.

> They call me Johnny F.
> I am the village souse.
> The Frater girls, my sisters,
> Live hidden in my house.

The sorrel passed slowly, calmly. The rider was swaying from side to side. He kept repeating his song over and over, not always in the same order. There were pauses between words, between sentences, some of them so long that he seemed to have stopped. Then he would go on with his monotonous ditty.

He passed very close, but he did not see us. Neither Brígido nor I said a word. We watched him move away in silence. What I had just heard was not new to me; I had always known it. But now I felt myself strangely shaken, as if I had glimpsed a mystery

adolescente de quince años eran verdaderamente revelaciones: cosas de mujeres, de hechizos y del amor.

Así estábamos cuando vimos acercarse a un jinete. No tardamos en reconocerlo. Era Juan P. Juan P. tenía un magnífico alazán. Era su orgullo y la envidia de los demás. Alto, brioso, elegante y tan gordo y reluciente como una taza de china. No había copetón en esas tierras que no había querido comprárselo o cambiárselo, pero Juan se había negado siempre con una sonrisa de interna satisfacción y un no sé qué de desprecio, aunque muy bien podría haber usado el dinero, pues mucha era la falta que le hacía.

Juan venía cantando; siempre cantaba cuando andaba borracho. Hoy no era excepción. Lo raro era lo que cantaba. Al principio no distinguíamos las palabras. Lo único discernible era lo gangoso y lo petulante de la voz, y naturalmente, lo desentonado. Por fin oímos la canción:

> A mí me llaman Juan P.
> Soy el borracho del pueblo.
> Tengo dos hermanas escondidas:
> Son las perrodas del pueblo.

El alazán iba paso a paso tranquilo. El jinete iba cimbreándose de lado a lado. Iba repitiendo su canción una y otra vez, no siempre en el mismo orden. Había pausas entre palabras, entre frases, algunas tan largas que parecía que había terminado, sólo para continuar su monótona cantinela.

Pasó muy cerca pero no nos vio. Ni Brígido ni yo dijimos nada. Nos quedamos viéndolo alejarse en silencio. Lo que acababa de oír no era nada nuevo para mí; siempre lo había sabido. Pero ahora me sentía extrañamente estremecido, como si percibiera un

behind that man, as if his familiar, innocuous words concealed a secret.

I had known John F. since childhood, and I always knew him by that name. I had seen his sisters many times, but since they were very peculiar and frightened me a little, I had never gone near them. I knew that everyone called them "the Fraters." Although I knew nothing of metathesis, I knew that the nickname was extremely offensive. I should mention here that I have not used true names. My reason for changing them will be obvious.

The name "Frater" had never concerned me. I had supposed vaguely that he was called John F. because of his reputation of being the town drunk and pariah. Crude people use a four-letter word beginning with *f* to express their scorn for such an individual. The name applied to the sisters, I had thought, was probably an extension of the brother's nickname which they had inherited. In all my life, I had never paid any attention to the fact that he never left the saloon, that the sisters went out only from their house to the church, that nobody spoke to them, that they wore dresses that had been out of style for many years, nor that all three bore an insulting name.

Now—I don't know why—I wanted to know what this was all about. And Brígido, at my insistence, told me the story behind the name, the drunkenness, the seclusion of the sisters.

John and his sisters came from one of the oldest families in the town. It was not a wealthy family, but comfortably well to do, as the tumble-down house in which they lived still testified. At the time of the event that produced the situation that exists today, the brother and sisters owned a good home, fertile farm lands, and enough cattle to live comfortably and with dignity.

John was a good-looking boy, kindly, gay, and hardworking.

misterio detrás de ese hombre, como si sus palabras inocuas y conocidas escondieran un secreto.

Yo conocía a Juan P. desde niño, y siempre lo conocí con ese nombre. Había visto a sus hermanas muchas veces, pero como eran muy raras y me daban un poco miedo, nunca me les había acercado. Y sabía que todo el mundo les decía "las perrodas". Aunque no supiera nada de metátesis sabía que el apodo era extremadamente ofensivo. Debo anotar aquí que no se llamaba Juan. Está visto por qué le he cambiado el nombre.

Nunca me había preocupado el nombre. Suponía vagamente que se le decía Juan P. por su condición de borracho. La plebe tenía un nombre para los borrachos que empezaba con "P". El nombre de las hermanas sería tal vez una extensión de la condición y del mote del hermano que ellas habían heredado. Que él no salía de las cantinas, que ellas salían sólo de la casa a la iglesia, que no le hablaban a nadie, que vestían estilos muchos años fuera de moda, que llevaban los tres un vil insulto de nombre, todo eso, me había tenido sin cuidado toda la vida.

Ahora, no sé por qué, quería saber. Y Brígido, a mis instancias, me contó la historia detrás del nombre, de la borrachera, de las hermanas encerradas.

Juan y sus hermanas procedían de una de las familias más antiguas del pueblo, no rica pero acomodada, como lo atestiguaba la casa destartalada en que aún vivían. Al desatarse el nudo que produjo la situación que hoy contemplamos, los tres hermanos tenían buena casa, buenos terrenos y bastante ganado para vivir holgadamente y con dignidad.

Juan era un buen mozo, bonachón, alegre y trabajador. No

There wasn't a girl in those valleys who would not have liked to marry him, and her parents would have been quite content with the choice.

The two sisters, whose names I shall not mention for reasons of delicacy, were very pretty. At the dances, the boys from all the nearby towns vied eagerly with one another for a chance to dance with them. They had already had several offers of marriage from boys considered the best catches of the region. But it seemed that they were in no hurry to get married. They were still quite young. They were having a very good time. And besides, their family life was unusually pleasant.

Fate intervened in an ironic manner in this promising situation. The brother and sisters were attending a wake for a neighbor. The whole town was there. Everyone was kneeling, praying the rosary before the body of the deceased.

The "Our Fathers", the "Hail, Mary's", and the "Mysteries" follow one another monotonously and interminably. Oh, how your knees and your middle and your back and your toes hurt when you pray the Rosary! And how that pain lasts and lasts when you pray with all the rococo flourishes and arabesques that are customary in my country! Men have the advantage in this kind of praying. When it becomes absolutely impossible, they change from one knee to the other. They put one hand on the floor to rest. They even sit back on their heels. And if it is necessary, they can get up and go out without being condemned to hell fire. On the other hand, tradition, decorum, and dignity demand that a woman keep herself as rigid as a board or a statue or a saint.

There are occasional pauses in which the leader of the prayer stops to produce a greater religious effect, or to catch his breath, or simply because he has forgotten what comes next or lost count

había chica por esos valles que no quisiera llevarlo a la misa determinante, y los padres de ellas habrían quedado muy contentos con la determinación.

Las dos hermanas, cuyos nombres no menciono por delicadeza, eran muy hermosas. En los bailes los jóvenes de todos los pueblos de la cercanía se desvivían, y hasta se desafiaban, por bailar con ellas. Habían tenido ya varias oftertas de matrimonio de los muchachos más valedores de la region. Pero parecía que ellas no tenían mucha prisa en casarse. Eran todavía muy jóvenes. Se estaban divirtiendo mucho. Y además, la vida familiar era más que agradable.

En esas condiciones, llenas de promesa, intervino el destino de una manera irónica. Asistían los hermanos a un velorio de un vecino. Todo el pueblo estaba allí. Estaban todos de rodillas rezando un *sudario* ante el cuerpo.

Los Padre Nuestros, los Ave Marías y los Misterios se seguían unos a los otros interminable y monótonamente. ¡Ay cómo duelen las rodillas, y la cintura, y la espalda y las puntas de los pies cuando se reza el rosario, y cómo dura cuando se reza con los arabescos y condecoraciones que se acostumbran en mi tierra! Los hombres llevan la ventaja en este suplicio. Cuando ya aquello se hace imposible cambian de una a otra rodilla. Ponen una mano en el suelo para descansar. Hasta se sientan en los talones. Y si es necesario pueden levantarse y salir sin ser condenados al infierno. La tradición, el decoro, la dignidad demandan que la mujer se mantenga rígida como una tabla, o una estatua, o una santa.

Hay unos silencios en que el rezador se detiene para producir el mayor efecto religioso, o para alcanzar el resuello, o simplemente porque se le ha olvidado lo que sigue o porque ha perdido la

of the "Hail, Mary's." Into one of those pauses, into the heavy silence, into that dense air burst a human explosion, private and shameful. It was one of those noises we all make but never in public. Even in private when they happen to us, they leave us somewhat demeaned, somewhat debased.

The horrified eyes of the entire congregation turned in the direction of the sound. They saw a woman rise, or, rather, draw herself up stiffly as if she were in her death agony. Everyone heard her scream, a hair-raising cry. A moment later she fell heavily to the floor, unconscious. It was one of John's sisters. The shock was tremendous. The only person present who did not shudder was the dead man.

What could have happened? Did she resist as long as was humanly possible and was the physical effort so great as to cause her to faint? Was it simply an accident? Did she swoon out of pure shame? Nobody knew for sure, no matter how long they discussed the subject. Of course the shamed family made no explanations.

Nobody made fun, nobody laughed that night. But later when the accident was mentioned, the riff-raff, the loafers, the foul-mouthed began to call the girl "the frater." As time went on, the same people applied the nickname to the entire family. Ever since, unpleasant people have called them "the Fraters." In John's case, they were satisfied with the initial letter. The gossip inevitably came to the ears of John and his sisters.

The silence of the grave fell upon the home of these unfortunates. The blinds went down and never rose again. The doors were always closed. The rose bushes, always so carefully tended, dried up. The wheat and alfalfa fields looked more neglected every day. The cattle must have been fed at night

cuenta de Ave Marías. En uno de esos silencios, en la quietud espesa, en la atmósfera densa, prorrumpe un explosión humana, individual y vergonzosa. Fue unos de esos ruidos que todos hacemos pero nunca en público. Aun en privado, cuando nos ocurren, nos dejan un poco rebajados, un poco envilecidos.

Todos los ojos de la congregación se volvieron en la dirección del sonido. Vieron alzarse una mujer, más bien estirarse, como en la agonía de la muerte. Todos la oyeron gritar, un grito horripilante. Un momento después caía desplomada al suelo, insensible. Era una de las hermanas de Juan. El escándalo fue tremendo. Sólo el difunto no se estremeció.

¿Qué pasaría? ¿Es que ella resistió todo lo que era humanamente posible y fue el esfuerzo físico el que le robó el sentido? ¿O fue simplemente un accidente? ¿Se desmayó de pura vergüenza? Nadie supo a ciencia cierta por mucho que se discutiera el tema. Claro que los hermanos nunca dijeron nada.

Nadie se burló, nadie se rió, esa noche. Pero ya otro día al comentarse el incidente, los holgazanes, los resolaneros, la plebe, empezaron a llamarle la Perroda, más tarde los mismos le aplicaron el mote a toda la familia. Desde entonces la gente de malas pulgas les llamó "los Perrodos". En el caso de Juan se conformaron con la inicial. No pudo menos que llegar a los oídos de Juan y sus hermanas.

El silencio de la tumba misma cayó sobre la casa de los hermanos. Bajaron las celosías y no volvieron a subir. Las puertas siempre cerradas. Se secaron los rosales, antes tan cuidadosamente atendidos. Los campos, trigales y alfalfares, se veían cada día más tristes, más abandonados. Los ganados debieron ser alimentados

because nobody ever saw the work being done. Relatives and neighbors tried to offer their services, but were repulsed. Gloom, solitude, and neglect invaded and took possession of their homestead.

After a while, after a long while, John went out into the street. At first he used to go only to the grocery store and back home immediately. Then he began to go to the saloon from time to time. As time passed, these visits increased in frequency. Finally, he never left the saloon. Always alone, taciturn, buried within himself. He drank and said nothing.

From time to time people heard that John had sold one more piece of land or more stock until they were all gone. The only thing he did not sell was his sorrel horse. It was as if he stuck to the horse as a symbol of the life that had been, of the life that might have been. And it was miraculous to watch how that horse protected the man, helplessly drunk, that he carried on his back.

At first the town riff-raff,—cowardly, despicable fellows,—left John alone. They watched him cautiously and respectfully, with good reasons, for John was capable of knocking them all to kingdom come. But as he kept losing control under the load of alcohol he carried, they kept growing bolder. The time came when they dared to throw the crude nickname in his face. John's rage and the strength it gave him were so great that the rats were badly frightened and scuttled away to their dens.

Since nothing had happened, the big, brave fellows had their own way next time. Little by little, in the drunken stupor in which he lived, John became accustomed to the nickname which the crude louts had applied to him. In his final decadence, he himself laughed idiotically at being John F., John Frater, and even

de noche porque nunca se vio a nadie haciéndolo. Los parientes y los vecinos quisieron prestar sus servicios y fueron rechazados. La tristeza, la soledad y el abandono invadieron le heredad y tomaron posesión de ella.

Por fin, después de mucho tiempo, Juan salió a la calle. Primero, sólo iba a la tienda y volvía pronto a su casa. Luego empezó a ir a la cantina de vez en cuando. Más tarde las visitas se hicieron más frecuentes. Finalmente no salía de la cantina. Siempre solo, taciturno, ensimismado. Bebía y callaba.

De vez en vez se oía que Juan había vendido un terreno más, o más reses, hasta que se acabaron. Sólo su caballo alazán no vendía. Era como si se atuviera a él como símbolo de la vida que fue, de la vida que pudo haber sido. Y era un milagro ver como aquel caballo parecía proteger al hombre incapacitado que llevaba encima.

Al principio los patanes del pueblo, gente ruin y cobarde, dejaban a Juan solo. Lo miraban con recelo y respeto, y bien hecho, porque Juan entonces era capaz de mandar a más de cuatro al quinto infierno. Pero a medida que Juan iba perdiendo los estribos con la carga de alcohol que llevaba encima se iban envalentonando ellos. Llegó el momento en que se atrevieron a echarle a la cara el vil apodo. La rabia de Juan fue tal, y la fuerza que de ella cobró, que las alimañas se llevaron un gran susto y se escurrieron a su madriguera.

La siguiente vez, como no había pasado nada, los valentones se salieron con la suya. Poco a poco Juan se fue acostumbrando, en el estupor en que vivía, al apodo que la plebe le había pegado, En su última decadencia él mismo se reía idiotizado de ser Juan P., Juan Perrodo y hasta quería, decían, ser digno del nombre que

wanted, or so they said, to be worthy of the name he had won. His life was a grotesque caricature. He accepted it and lived it.

Brígido stopped talking and after a silence moved off in the direction of the carriage house where Abraham and Epimenio were storing great blocks of ice in sawdust for the still distant summer.

Later, I saw the beautiful sorrel horse return with his shapeless human burden. He was going to the house with the drawn blinds, the house where fifty-year-old women still lived in seclusion. I began to chop wood furiously. In each log I saw the stupid face of an abusive brute that had condemned three human beings to the hell of that life, who had poisoned a clean family with their filthy breath. With vengeful pleasure I split the faces and reduced to chips and splinters those unfeeling men whom I knew.

I cut wood all afternoon like a crazy man. The mound, the promontory of my house grew rapidly with the mental and bucal filth of men. If you pass through Tierra Amarilla nowadays, notice the hillock at my house. If you scratch around a little, you will find there eyes and tongues and human brains. They belong to the ones who gave the "Fraters" their name. Those eyes and those tongues and those brains must be there. I left them there.

había ganado. Su vida era una grotesca caricatura. La aceptó y la vivió.

Brígido acabó de hablar y después de un silencio se alejó en la dirección de la cochera donde Abraham y Epimenio estaban guardando grandes bloques de hielo en aserrín para el verano aún muy lejano.

Más tarde vi volver el hermoso caballo alazán con su carga humana e informe. Iba a la casa de las celosías, la casa de las mujeres cincuentonas que allí existían. Me puse a partir leña con furia. En cada leño veía yo la cara boba de un hombre abusivo y bruto que había condenado a tres seres humanos al infierno de esta vida, que había envenenado con su aliento asqueroso a una familia limpia. Con qué gusto les rajé la cara, y la hice astillas y briznas, a los hombres insensibles que yo conocía.

Partí leña como un loco. El montón, el promontorio de mi casa creció aquella tarde con la inmundicia de la mente y la lengua de los hombres. Y si ustedes pasan hoy por Tierra Amarilla fíjense en el montón de mi casa. Si escarban poco hallarán allí ojos y lenguas y sesos humanos. Son los de los que bautizaron a "los Perrodos." Allí tienen que estar. Allí los dejé yo.

GET THAT STRAIGHT

Don José Viejo (Old Mister Joe) was more ancient than hunger. He was so tiny and so fragile that it hurt you to look at him. The sun or old age or knowledge of life had burned his skin till it was almost black. He shambled around town with his hat pulled down over his ears and his shoulders hunched forward, moving with tiny steps that reminded me of the hopping of birds. Everyone called him Don José Viejo.

On the street, loafers, louts, and children left him strictly alone. The old fellow was sharp and had a tongue of such razor-edged steel that several smart alecks had found themselves pinned to the wall and bleeding, the butt of the jokes and laughter of their companions, without even knowing how it happened. Everybody

Sábelo

Don José Viejo era más viejo que el hambre. Era tan pequeñito y tan frágil que daba lástima verlo. El sol o la edad o la verdad de la vida le había quemado la piel y era casi prieto. Andaba por el pueblo con el sombrero calado hasta las orejas, un poco jorobado, con unos pasitos que me hacían pensar en los pájaros. Todos le decían don José Viejo.

Los ociosos, los malcriados y los niños lo dejaban solo porque el viejito era tan listo y tenía una lengua de tan refinado metal que varios atrevidos se habían hallado clavados y sangrando en la pared sin saber ni cómo, expuestos a las burlas y risas de sus compañeros. Esto todo el mundo lo sabía. Esto lo sabía el anciano también. Tenía el paso abierto por dondequiera que andaba.

knew this. The old man knew it, too. He had open passage wherever he went.

I don't remember that he had any family. He lived alone in a miserable little hut that was cleaner than the bones of the desert. And he dressed fairly well—I don't know how. I remember that many times the old fellow invited me to his house and gave me meat pies, sugared cheese, jerky, and other things that the children of my time liked very much. Sometimes he told me stories of the old days, stories of Indians, of wild beasts in the forest, of cowboys.

On one occasion, he told me how he had fought a bear hand to hand. How, being so small, he had curled himself up under one arm of the monster so that the animal could neither crush nor bite him. How from underneath he had thrust his knife again and again into the belly of the brute until it fell. A nine-year-old boy listening in open-mouthed amazement, I believed everything he told me. It was not necessary that he should prove his story. However, moved by some obscure impulse, Mister Joe took off his shirt and showed me his back. Today, after so many years, I still remember with frightening clarity the scars he bore. The claw marks, where the bear had torn away the living flesh, were indicated by several series of four irregular lines. It was a grillwork of scars. From that day on, I had an almost religious respect for Mister Joe.

Old Mister Joe used to come to my house every day, always carrying a little pail. My mother gave him a daily bucket of milk, for we had more than we needed. Perhaps it was because the old man was so kind to me, or because he had once been one of our shepherds, or simply because he was Mister Joe. I never knew why.

No recuerdo que tuviera familia. Vivía solo en una choza de mala muerte pero más limpia que los huesos del desierto. Y se las arreglaba bastante bien no sé cómo. Yo me acuerdo de muchas veces que el viejito me invitó a su casa y me regaló empanadas, queso con azúcar, carne seca y otras cosas que a los niños de mi tiempo nos gustaban mucho. Algunas veces me contaba cuentos de cuando hay (así les llamábamos a los cuentos de tiempos remotos): cuentos de indios, de las fieras del bosque, de vaqueros.

En una ocasión me contó cómo había luchado mano a mano con un oso. Cómo, siendo tan pequeño, se había acurrucado dentro del abrazo del monstruo de tal manera que la fiera no podía ni apretarlo ni morderlo. Cómo, por debajo le había metido el cuchillo una y otra vez en las entrañas hasta que el bruto cayó. Yo, niño de nueve años, me creí embobado todo lo que me dijo. No era necesario que el viejito me lo documentara. Pero, movido por no sé qué impulsos, don José Viejo se quitó la camisa y me mostró la espalda. Hoy, después de tantos años, recuerdo con espantosa claridad las cicatrices que tenía. En series de cuatro rayas irregulares estaban marcados allí los arañazos del oso donde le había arrancado la carne viva. Una parrilla de cicatrices. Desde ese día yo tuve para don José Viejo un respeto casi religioso.

Venía don José Viejo a mi casa todos los días, siempre con su cubeta en la mano. Mi madre le regalaba un cubo de leche todos los días, ya que a nosotros nos sobraba. Tal vez porque el viejito era tan generoso conmigo, o porque antes había sido pastor nuestro, o simplemente por ser don José Viejo. Yo nunca supe por qué.

At that time we had a great many bees. The bee hives were on a bank beside the alfalfa field, because people said the best honey came from alfalfa blossoms. The hives could be clearly seen from the kitchen window. When the time came to gather the honey, the workmen put on two pairs of trousers, a jacket, and thick gloves. On their heads, they wore something like a bucket of woven wire. They looked like real monsters. A black cloud emerged as they uncovered the hives and buzzed about them all the time they were filling the buckets they carried. I watched them from a distance, very much impressed.

One winter a friend and I were out hunting birds with our slingshots. The ground was covered with frozen snow, so that we could walk on its surface. We found ourselves near the beehives. The idea occurred to us to go and eat some honey. I don't remember whether the big boxes were left out every winter or whether this was unusual.

When we got quite close, we stopped with some apprehension, for we knew very well what the bees could do. We discussed the situation for a while and decided that the bees must either be numbed by the cold or asleep, for everything was quiet.

I was the one who opened the box. Taking off the top, hearing the menacing buzz, and seeing the swarm were all one. Instantly the black, pointed cloud surged from the mouth of the hive and headed straight for the intruders, already in precipitate flight. The force of our pounding feet broke through the frozen snow which had supported us before, and we sank up to our belts. We kept running and struggling in despair, victims of a panic terror.

From time to time, I gave a quick glance over my shoulder without daring to take a good look. The sight of the thick black threat made me redouble my efforts. I don't know how long it

Teníamos entonces muchas abejas. Los abejares estaban en una lomita al lado de los alfalfares porque, según decían, de allí venía la mejor miel. De la ventana de la cocina se veían perfectamente. Cuando llegaba el momento de recoger la miel los criados se ponían dos pantalones encimados, chaqueta y guantes gruesos, y sobre la cabeza uno como cubo de alambre tejido. Parecían verdaderos monstruos. Al destapar las cajas salía una nube negra que zumbaba alrededor de ellos mientras llenaban los cubos que llevaban. Yo los cuidaba desde lejos, muy impresionado.

Un invierno un amiguito y yo andábamos cazando pájaros con nuestras hondas. Había nieve y estaba helada, de modo que podíamos andar sobre la superficie. Andábamos cerca de las cajas de las abejas. Se nos ocurrió ir y comer miel. No recuerdo ahora si se dejaban allí los cajones todos los inviernos o si esto era extraordinario.

Al acercarnos nos detuvimos con algún recelo ya que los dos sabíamos muy bien lo que las abejas podían hacer. Discutimos la situación un rato y decidimos que las abejas estarían entumidas o dormidas. Todo estaba en silencio. Todo parecía muerto.

Yo fui el que abrí la caja. Destapar la caja y oír el zumbido y ver el hervidero de las abejas fue todo uno. En seguida se alzó de la boca de la caja la nube negra, hecha punta, dirigida hacia nosotros, ya en precipitada fuga. La nieve helada que antes nos había soportado ahora se vencía con la fuerza de nuestros saltos y nos hundíamos hasta la cintura. Corríamos desolados, víctimas de un pánico espantoso.

De vez en cuando miraba yo de reojo sobre el hombro, sin atreverme a mirar de lleno y veía la espesa amenaza negra y redoblaba mis esfuerzos. No sé cuánto tardaríamos en darnos

took us to realize that the bees were not overtaking us. Perhaps it was when we fell exhausted in a drift.

We saw then that the mobile black cloud had descended and was lying motionless on the snow. When they came in contact with the cold air, the bees had become sluggish, then numb, and had finally fallen on the white, inhospitable surface.

We were a long time understanding what had happened and even longer in recognizing and admitting what a cruel thing we had done. There, scattered over the snow like raisins in rice, were the dead or dying bees. My first impulse was to gather them up and put them back into the hives, but it was obviously too late for that.

We did not say anything. We went back home in silence. Over the surface of the snow again. Honey, birds, and slings were forgotten. I did not look at my friend. He did not look at me. I suspect that it was because we both had something to hide. Out of the corner of my eye, I saw him dig at his eyes with the thick sleeve of his winter jacket. My wet cheeks were burning in the cold afternoon breeze.

Old Mister Joe visited the beehives, too. We used to see him pass with his little pail. He went to the hives, helped himself, and came back with the pail full. I am sure he did not have permission, but, as I said, the old fellow had, or assumed, special privileges. Since the loss was so insignificant, and since we would have given him the honey anyway, my father let him alone.

I already had a somewhat superstitious veneration for Mister Joe on account of his conquering bears and knowing so many unusual things. But the thing that astonished me most was that the bees did not sting him. I had seen him among the hives without any protection at all, tranquilly filling his pail while the dizzying

cuenta de que las abejas no nos alcanzaban, tal vez cuando caímos rendidos sobre la nieve.

Vimos entonces que la móvil mancha negra había descendido y ahora yacía inmóvil sobre la nieve. Al ponerse en contacto con el aire frío las abejas se entorpecían, se entumecían y caían vencidas sobre el suelo blanco e inhospitable.

Tardamos en comprender lo que había pasado, y aún más en reconocer y admitir la maldad y la crueldad de lo que acabábamos de hacer. Allí, salpicadas sobre la nieve, como pasas en el arroz, estaban las abejas muertas o muriéndose. Mi primer impulso fue recogerlas y devolverlas a la colmena, pero estaba visto que ya era tarde para eso.

No decíamos nada. En silencio volvimos a casa. Sobre la superficie de la nieve otra vez. La miel, las hondas y los pájaros olvidados. Yo no miraba a mi amigo. El no me miraba a mí. Sospecho que era porque ambos teníamos algo que ocultar. Por el rabo del ojo lo vi tallarse los ojos con la manga gruesa de su chaqueta de invierno. A mí me ardían las mejillas húmedas en la brisa fría de la tarde.

Don José Viejo también visitaba las colmenas. Lo veíamos pasar con su cubeta. Iba y se surtía y volvía con la cubeta llena. No creo que tuviera la venia, pero como ya he dicho, el viejito tenía o se usurpaba derechos especiales. Como la pérdida era tan insignificante, y en todo caso se le habría regalado, mi padre lo dejaba.

Yo ya le tenía un acatamiento un tanto supersticioso a don José Viejo por ser un domador de osos y por saber tantas cosas extraordinarias. Pero lo que me maravillaba aún más era que no le picaban las abejas. Yo lo había visto entre las colmenas, sin protección alguna, el enjambre vertiginoso zumbándole alrededor

swarm buzzed around his ears and the individual bees crawled over his hands and face. It seemed to me that he was talking to them. When his task was finished, he moved away with his birdlike step, absolutely calm.

This was a tremendous mystery for me. I used to wonder what quality of this man made it possible for him to face such terror and come out unscathed. This fact perplexed me even more than the business of the bear because I had had experience with bees. I speculated on the matter without ever reaching a solution. If I asked my father or the workmen, they would tell me that there are people like that. A statement which would tell me nothing at all.

One day when the old man came for milk, I was carried away by uncontrollable curiosity. Curbing the fear I had of him—as I have said the old fellow had an acid tongue—I decided to put the question to him.

"Listen, Don José, why don't the bees sting you?" I was very careful to omit the "Viejo."

"Well, boy, what do you think?"

"I don't know. I only know that they sting me and everybody else."

"I'd like to tell you, son. But it is a secret. Get that straight!"

"If you'll tell me, I won't tell anybody. I swear I won't. I'll swear on the Bible."

"Don't take holy things in vain, you bad-mannered brat!"

"Don't be mad, Don José. It is just that I wanted. . . ."

"All right, boy. But be very careful. . . . Do you really promise to keep the secret? You won't tell anyone, not even your father?"

"You can count on me, Don José." I felt very grown-up.

"Well, I'll tell you the truth. But I warn you that if you tell a

de los oídos, las abejas trepándosele por las manos y la cara, y él tranquilamente llenando su cubeta. A mí me parecía que hablaba con ellas. Terminada su tarea se alejaba a paso de pájaro con una calma absoluta.

Esto era un tremendo misterio para mí. Yo me preguntaba cuál sería la virtud de este hombre que le permitía entrar en la boca del miedo y salir ileso. Era esto para mí aún más intrigante que lo del oso porque en este terreno yo tenía experiencia. Yo fantaseaba sin llegar a ninguna solución. Si le preguntaba a mi padre o a alguno de los peones sólo me decían que había gente así. Lo cual no me decía nada.

Un día que vino el anciano por la leche, llevado por una curiosidad que ya no podía resistir, y dominando el miedo que le tenía, porque ya he dicho que el viejito era picante, me decidí a preguntárselo a él mismo.

—Oigame, don José, ¿y a usted por qué no le pican las abejas?— Me cuidé muy bien de omitir el "Viejo."

—Pues, hombre, ¿y tú qué crees?

—Yo no sé. Yo sólo sé que a mí y a todos los demás sí nos pican.

—Hijo, quisiera decirte, pero es un secreto. Sábelo.

—Si me lo dice a mí, yo no le digo a nadie. Por Dios Santito.

—No jures en vano, malcriado.

—No se enoje, don José, si es que quería . . .

—Está bien, muchacho. Pero mucho cuidado . . . ¿De veras me prometes guardar el secreto? ¿No le dirás a nadie, ni a tu papá siquiera?

—Don José, usted puede contar conmigo.—Me senti muy hombre.

—Pues te voy a decir la verdad. Pero te advierto que si tú

single word of what I am going to say, the people of the valley will kill me. Then all the bees in the valley and the forest—and there are millions—will leave their hives and come down on Tierra Amarilla like a fury to finish off all the people. Nothing will be left but bones. All that will happen because I am a bee. Get that straight!" His little eyes were dancing with glee.

"Don José Vie—I mean Don José. . . ." I had already repented of my action, but I did not know how to get out of the situation. The old man was off; there was no way to stop him.

"A long time ago, a fine, lively young fellow lived in a nearby town. There were two strange things about him. He was unusually fond of honey, and he loved bees. He liked them so much that he suffered a lot because men held them prisoners and stole their honey from them. Get that straight!

"The young man used to visit the bees and talk to them. Little by little he began to learn their language. They became great friends. He used to take them the most beautiful flowers from the garden, and they gave him the sweetest and richest honey anybody has ever seen.

"One day he took a notion to set his friends free. Get that straight! He began to whistle a strange melody, which the bees understood very well, and started out for the forest. The bees left their hives; they abandoned the alfalfa and the flowers and followed him, all humming the unusual melody that the young man was whistling. The world of men was filled with sound, shadow, and fear.

"The young man searched out the most hidden spot in the forest and there, in a tree which seemed suitable, he hived the bees. After that, he used to go from town to town whistling that same melody until there wasn't a single prisoner bee—get that!—in all this

cuentas una sola palabra de lo que yo te voy a decir, la gente del pueblo me matará, y entonces todas las abejas del valle y del bosque, y hay millones, saldrán de sus colmenas y descenderán sobre Tierra Amarilla como una furia y acabarán con la gente. No quedarán ni los huesos. Todo esto pasará porque yo soy abeja, sábelo.—Los ojitos le bailaban con alegría.

—Don José Vie—, es decir, don José . . .—Ya me había arrepentido pero no sabía como salirme del trance. El viejito estaba lanzado; ya no había manera de detenerlo.

—Hace muchos años en un pueblo cercano vivía un joven muy bueno y muy alegre. Tenía dos rarezas. Le gustaba mucho la miel y quería mucho a las abejas, sábelo. Las quería tanto que sufría mucho porque los hombres las tenían prisioneras y les robaban la miel.

—Sábelo. Ese joven iba a las colmenas y les hablaba y poco a poco fue aprendiendo su lengua. Se hicieron muy amigos. El les traía las flores más hermosas del jardín, y ellas le regalaban la miel más dulce y más rica que han conocido los hombres.

Un día se le antojó poner a sus amigas en libertad. Empezó a silbar una melodía muy extraña que las abejas comprendían muy bien y se dirigió al bosque. Las abejas se salieron de las colmenas, abandonaron las flores y las alfalfas y lo siguieron, zumbando todas la inusitada melodía que silbaba el joven. El mundo de los hombres se llenó de sonido, de sombra y de temor.

El joven buscó el sitio más recóndito del bosque, y allí en el árbol que le pareció adecuado, enjambró a las abejas. Después iba de pueblo en pueblo silbando la misma melodía hasta que no había una sola abeja prisionera, sábelo, en todas estas tierras. Por

country. For many, many years there was no honey for toast nor for colds and coughs in the world of men.

"As you know, bees have a queen, the mother of all the bees. She is the biggest and most beautiful of them all. Well—now get this!—the queen fell in love with the young man. One day she settled on his lips and kissed him. So the young man became a bee and married the queen. And he died because the lovers of the queen must always die. Get that straight.

"That young man was my father. The queen bee was my mother. I was born in the forest among the bees. They brought me up. I am their brother. Get that straight! If you had looked closely, you would have seen the two little wings I have on my back. Look at me now and you will see that I look like a bee." And he was right!

"Now you understand why the bees don't sting me, why I talk to them. Now you'll understand the scars I have on my back. Bears are my worst enemies. They have followed me all my life. They want to suck my blood. They know what no man in the world knows—now get this!—that I do not have blood in my veins. They know that I am a bee and have honey instead."

The great bee rose from his perch. He picked up his bucket of milk. He fixed me with a beelike gaze.

"Remember, boy, what I told you. Not a single word! Get that straight!"

He went away with his tiny steps. I sat there trembling. I knew that Don José Viejo never lied.

muchos años no hubo miel para el pan tostado, no hubo miel para los resfriados en el mundo de los hombres.

—Como tú sabes, las abejas tienen reina, la abeja madre. Es la más grande y más bella de todas ellas. Pues, sábelo, la reina se enamoró del joven. Un día se le paró en los labios y lo besó. Y el joven se volvió abeja y se casó con la reina. Y se murió, sábelo, pues los amores de las reinas son mortales.

—Ese joven fue mi padre. La reina fue mi madre. Yo nací en el bosque entre las abejas. Sábelo. Ellas me criaron. Soy abeja. Soy su hermano. Si te hubieras fijado, habrías visto las alitas que tengo en la espalda. Fíjate ahora y verás que parezco abeja. —Y tenía razón. . .

—Ahora podrás comprender por qué no me pican las abejas, por qué les hablo. Además ahora te podrás explicar las cicatrices que tengo en la espalda. Los osos son mis peores enemigos. Toda mi vida me han perseguido. Quieren chuparme la sangre, sábelo. Ellos saben lo que no sabe nadie, que yo no tengo sangre en las venas, que yo soy abeja y tengo miel en las venas. Sábelo.

El abejonazo se levantó de donde estaba sentado. Recogió su cubeta de leche. Me clavó en el aire con una mirada abejuna.

—Acuérdate, muchacho, de lo que te dije. Ni una sola palabra. Sábelo.

Se alejó, pasito a pasito. Yo me quedé temblando. Yo sabía que don José Viejo no mentía.

FORGE WITHOUT FIRE

Edumenio's blacksmith shop was the most fascinating place in the world to me when I was nine years old. There, ardently busy, I spent many long hours of idleness. On my way home from school in the afternoons, I always stopped for a short while—some times for a long while, which I later found hard to explain at home. Other boys devoted to the same interests joined me there.

The attraction was a double one. The smithy itself and Edumenio. He was a brawny man, rather tall and heavyset, who spoke little. A lock of almost blonde hair kept continually falling down over his right eye when he was working. He shook it back occasionally with violent jerks of his head like a horse that is scaring away a fly or pushed at it at times with the back of his

La fragua sin fuego

La fragua de Edumenio era el sitio más interesante para mí cuando yo tenía nueve años. Allí pasaba yo muchos y largos ratos de ocio, fervorosamente ocupado. Al volver del colegio por las tardes siempre me detenía un poco, algunas veces un mucho, que después me costaba trabajo explicar en casa. Otros chicos se reunían allí conmigo con la misma dedicación.

El atractivo era doble. La fragua misma y Edumenio. Era éste un hombre robusto, más bien alto y ancho, y taciturno. Un mechón casi rubio le caía de continuo sobre el ojo derecho mientras trabajaba que él sacudía una y otra vez con unas cabezadas violentas algo así como un caballo que espanta una mosca, o a veces se lo retiraba con el dorso de la mano sudorosa. Su cara

sweaty hand. Down his round, white face, which almost always glowed from the heat of the fire or the violence of his own efforts, rivulets of sweat and soot started that continued downward and were lost in a chest like that of a pagan god beneath the soaked and ragged shirt. His bare arms, burned a reddish bronze, were worthy, if not capable, of taking over the task of Atlas. His huge hands were pitted with burns and cracks resulting from his work. He always wore a leather apron tightly cinched around a surprisingly small waist.

Edumenio almost never spoke. And when he spoke, he did not say much. He hummed to himself. He whistled to himself. He muttered to himself. When we saw him thus buried in his own thoughts, we were very careful not to interrupt. We realized, without knowing how, that this communion was something very private. Besides, he had a way of frowning that frightened us. His eyes fixed on a distant spot and on an invisible person. A vague smile that appeared and disappeared. The contrast between the serenity, almost sweetness, of that face in a state of repose and the fury with which he worked was something to see. He hammered with a ferocity that filled the shop with the shrieks of wounded iron, with tears of light, and with the fusillade with which the dying iron defended itself. He roused the coals to leaping rage by pricking them in the face with fiery metals. The smoke of the battle covered and begrimed us all. That is the way Edumenio was: great peace and great belligerence.

At that time, of course, I could not have explained the attraction that drew me there so frequently. Perhaps that rare mixture of deep serenity and erupting violence, of spirit and beast, gave me a sensation of being in the presence of a complete man. Perhaps it was pride that he would allow me to be there or a desire

blanca y llena, casi siempre encendida por el calor del fuego o la violencia del esfuerzo, tenía surcos de sudor y tizne que se perdían en el pecho de dios pagano bajo la empapada camisa harapienta. Sus brazos desnudos desde el hombro, bronceados hasta el rojo, eran dignos, si no capaces, de sostener el mundo. Sus manos vastas estaban picadas de quemaduras y grietas propias del oficio. Llevaba un delantal de cuero fuertemente ceñido a la cintura, sorprendentemente pequeña.

Edumenio casi nunca hablaba. Y cuando hablaba no hablaba mucho. Canturreaba para sí. Silbaba para sí. Murmuraba para sí. Nosotros cuando lo veíamos así ensimismado teníamos mucho cuidado de no interrumpir. Nos dábamos cuenta sin saber cómo que aquello era algo muy íntimo. Además, él tenía una manera de fruncir el ceño que nos daba miedo. Los ojos puestos en una parte y en una persona ausentes. Una vaga sonrisa que aparecía y desaparecía. Era de ver, porque curioso era, el contraste entre la placidez, casi dulzura, de aquella cara en estado de trance y la furia con que trabajaba. Martillaba con una ferocidad que llenaba la fragua de gritos del hierro herido, de las lágrimas de luz y de la metralla con que el moribundo hierro se defendía. Hacía rabiar a las brasas picándoles la cara con metales vivos. El humo de la batalla nos cubría y nos manchaba a todos. Así era Edumenio: mucha paz y mucha guerra.

Yo, claro, no habría podido entonces explicar la querencia que allí me llevaba con tanta frecuencia. Quizá esa rara mezcla de fuerte serenidad y violencia encabritada, de alma y animal, me darían la sensación de estar en la presencia de todo un hombre, el orgullo de que él me lo permitiera, el deseo de ser como él. No

to be like him. I don't know. One thing I am sure of, however. When he hit himself with a hammer once in a while, when he burned himself, or when something turned out wrong, he burst out with powerful oaths, the kind that surge upward and stick to the ceiling of the house or the ceiling of the world, where they hang, dripping poison and fire. I felt a curious secret pleasure when this happened. I felt myself sharing the strength of that man, worthy for a moment of entering the mysterious grown-up world. I knew by memory all his strong words and curses, and, with a joy and affection I have rarely been able to achieve in my life, I kept them deep inside me in a little hidden box. I remember that on rare occasions, when I was alone, I would take them out to admire them. For a long time, they were my richest possessions. Even today I still have a few which I take out to flash on special occasions. It was a curious thing—I never said those words. Perhaps it was because it seemed a sacrilege to do so.

Edumenio was very good to us. He fixed our broken toys. He made us tops with points as sharp as swords. He used to do marvels with a sheet of tin. He gave us barrel hoops, tiles, and other bits of trash that children like so much. And he let us do things ourselves. We hammered, we pounded, we drove nails, giving free rein to our constructive and destructive desires. But the most wonderful thing of all was that we could get ourselves good and dirty. The child who has never gotten very grimy very often has had a false and incomplete childhood. Another thing. He never treated us with the condescension which most adults have for children. He talked to us man to man. We swelled with importance when we could help him some way—bring him a tool, revive the forge fire with the bellows, go out to buy him some cigarettes.

sé. Lo cierto es que de vez en vez, cuando se daba un martillazo, cuando se quemaba o algo le salía tuerto soltaba unos *sacres*, de esos que suben y se pegan en los cielos de las casas o en el cielo del mundo y de allí chorrean gotitas de veneno y de fuego. Yo sentía un curioso placer secreto, me sentía partícipe de la fuerza de ese hombre, digno por un momento de entrar en el mundo misterioso de los hombres. Yo me sabía todas sus palabrotas y blasfemias y me las guardaba allá muy adentro en una cajita escondida con un gozo y un cariño que muy pocas veces he podido captar en mi vida. Recuerdo que a veces, no muchas, cuando estaba solo, las sacaba para admirarlas. Fueron por mucho tiempo de mis posesiones más ricas. Todavía hoy conservo algunas que sólo saco a relucir en ocasiones especiales. Cosa curiosa—yo nunca las dije. Tal vez sería porque me parecía sacrílego.

Era muy bueno. Nos componía los juguetes rotos. Nos hacía trompos con unas puntas como espadas. Hacía maravillas con hoja de lata. Nos daba aros, tejas, y mil piezas de desperdicio que a los niños les gustan tanto. Nos dejaba hacer. Martillábamos, machacábamos, clavábamos, y le dábamos rienda suelta a nuestro afán de construir y destruir. Pero el colmo de las delicias era que nos podíamos tiznar. El niño que no se haya tiznado mucho y muchas veces, ha tenido una niñez falsa e incompleta. Otra cosa. Nunca nos trató con esa condescendencia que tienen los mayores para los niños. Nos hablaba de hombre a hombre. Cuando podíamos ayudarle en algo, traerle una herramienta, animar el brasero con el fuelle, ir a comprarle unos cigarros, eso nos llenaba de importancia.

Sometimes when there was nothing to do or when he was loafing on the porch of his little house, we used to sit down in the shade or the sun, according to the season. He in the center and we boys around him, as close as we could get. Everybody quiet. We proud of sharing this communion of manly silence. He lost in his meditations but without forgetting us. Occasionally, he tied somebody's shoe, blew another's nose, or constructed some small miracle for us. I used to feel a strange fulfillment in those silences, a thoroughly pleasant relaxation. Suddenly, he would stand up and, looking down on us from his great height, start pulling us to our feet as if we were feathers. With a pat on the bottom, he would send us on our way with a laconic, "Time to go home, kids" or something of the kind. I used to go away, strolling or running, but always with something of the pleasure the forge and the man had given me that day and, of course, with a lot of soot and grime.

He had a little white house with a balustraded porch. In the whole town, there wasn't a cleaner, better ordered house, inside and out, than Edumenio's. His little garden was beautiful. He had hollyhocks, Castilian roses, and other flowers whose names I don't remember or never knew. He lived there alone and took care of everything alone. He did his own cooking, washing, and ironing. He certainly must have had a story and a family, but I never knew anything about that.

He had the custom, when he came home, of undressing to the waist and soaping his entire upper body. Then he would wash noisily and vigorously, scattering water all over the place. I tried to imitate this custom at home with unfortunate results. Then he would put on a white shirt. Since he himself had washed and ironed it, he deserved credit for that. I suppose that on other

A veces, cuando no había que hacer, o de tardeada en el portal de su casita, nos sentábamos a la sombra o en la resolana, según era indicado. El en el centro y nosotros alrededor de él, al cual más cerca se podía meter. Todos sin hablar. Nosotros orgullosos de compartir esta comunión de silencio varonil. El perdido en sus cavilaciones pero sin abandonarnos. Ya le ataba el zapato a uno, ya le sonaba la nariz a otro, ya nos construía algun pequeño milagro. En esos silencios yo sentía una extraña plenitud, una holganza en todo grata. De pronto se incorporaba y mirándonos desde su altura nos iba poniendo de pie uno a uno como si fuéramos unas plumas, y con una nalgada en el trasero nos enviaba a casa con un lacónico, "Chavales a la casa." O algo parecido. Yo me iba, andando o corriendo, pero siempre conservando algo del placer que la fragua y el hombre me habían dado ese día, y desde luego, mucho tizne.

Tenía una casita blanca con portal y barandal. No había en el pueblo casa más limpia y mejor arreglada, por dentro y por fuera, que la de Edumenio. Su jardincito era el más pulcro; tenía varas de San José, rosas de Castilla, y otras cuyo nombre no recuerdo o nunca supe. Allí vivía solo y se las arreglaba solo. Cocinaba, lavaba, planchaba. De seguro tuvo historia y tuvo familia, pero de eso yo nunca supe nada.

Tenía la costumbre cuando volvía a casa de desnudarse hasta la cintura y enjabonarse medio cuerpo, después lavarse con estruendo y vehemencia, salpicando agua por todas partes. Yo quise imitar esto en mi casa con mala fortuna. Luego se ponía una camisa blanca. Siendo que él mismo lavaba y planchaba, esto tenía mérito. Me supongo que en otras ocasiones se bañaba la otra

occasions he bathed the other half of his body, but I can't testify to that, since I never saw it happen.

Every two or three months, when least expected, the forge failed to open and remained closed for one, even two weeks. People said that Edumenio went to the city, got himself gloriously drunk, and abandoned himself completely to sex and sin. This was curious because in our town nobody ever saw him take a drink. He never went to the bar nor to dances. He had no dealings with women, good or bad. At the age of nine, I had absolutely no use for girls. Perhaps that is why we understood one another so well.

When he returned from those trips, he came back with a big grouch on. He could not even stand himself. I would see the smithy open and hear the hammering inside, but I would not go near. I waited about three days, and then I went. Our curious friendship began again without questions, without explanations— only friendship.

He came back from one of those trips with a companion. Happy, talkative, laughing. Edumenio had gotten married. The news flashed through the town. When I learned about it, I felt a vague fear that things were going to change, that the smithy would no longer be the same.

Her name was Henrietta. From the first time I saw her, I was convinced that she was the most beautiful creature God had ever put on earth. I soon decided that her laughter was the most musical, her voice the merriest in the whole world. I did not know it, but I was madly in love with her. It was my first love affair.

Many boys fall in love with their teachers. That road was always closed to me. My teachers were nuns. And who is going to fall in love with a nun? Especially a boy who carried around a little hidden box of bad words. Later I have seen some sisters who

mitad del cuerpo, pero de esto no puedo dar testimonio porque nunca lo vi.

Cada dos o tres meses, el día menos pensado, la fragua no se abría y permanecía cerrada por una y hasta dos semanas. Decían que Edumenio se iba a la ciudad y se ponía una borrachera imperial y se entregaba por completo al mal andar. Esto era curioso porque en el pueblo no le vio nadie tomar un trago nunca. No iba a la cantina ni a los bailes. De mujeres, nada—ni buenas ni malas. Yo, a mis nueve años, no quería a las chicas ni pintadas. Quizá por eso nos entendíamos tan bien.

Cuando volvía de estos viajes volvía con las muelas al revés. No se aguantaba ni solo. Yo veía la fragua abierta y oía los martillazos dentro, pero no me acercaba. Esperaba unos tres días y luego iba a la fragua. Empezaba otra vez nuestra curiosa amistad—sin preguntas, sin explicaciones—solo amistad.

En uno de esos viajes volvió acompañado. Alegre, locuaz y risueño. Edumenio se había casado. La voz corrió por el pueblo. Cuando yo supe sentí un vago temor de que las cosas iban a cambiar, que ya no sería lo mismo en la fragua.

Se llamaba Henriqueta. Desde que la vi la primera vez quedé convencido que era la criatura más hermosa que Dios había puesto en la tierra. Pronto decidí que su risa era la más musical, su voz la más risueña de todo el mundo. Yo no lo sabía, pero estaba locamente enamorado. Estaba experimentando mi primer amor.

Muchos niños se enamoran de sus maestras. Ese camino estuvo siempre cerrado para mí. Mis maestras fueron monjas. Y ¿quién se va a enamorar de una monja? Especialmente un niño que lleva escondida una cajita de malas palabras. Más tarde he visto a

awoke a somewhat more than casual interest in me, but it was not that way when I was a boy. That is why I came to love a little late in life, and perhaps for that reason my surrender was complete.

I used to watch her with calf's eyes in a lamb's face, and I followed her like a dog. It was a love that asks nothing and gives everything—intelligence, will power, strength. A love without merchandising, without trade, without pounds of flesh or vials of fragrance, without barter of secret effusions. Without collections, calculations, or receipts. A clean, pure, new love without hands, nor words, nor lips. Mute and secret, it neither comes nor goes. It is fixed nowhere; it only *is*. It never reaches realization. It is like the quiet air that never becomes an impure wind. There is no vanity. There is no narcissism. It is all sweet, throbbing pain. It is a love that is death without desires or hopes of being reborn. Love must kill, to a greater or lesser degree. If it does not kill, it is not love; it is something else. Only a child is capable of complete love.

Edumenio was not the same any more. He was now the most jovial fellow in the district. Roars of laughter, backslapping for anyone who came near him, and a frightening tendency to run off at the mouth. Now when he played with us, he pretended to be a bull or got down on all fours to play horse. Jokes and teasing. His songs, at full lung power, silenced the wails and moans of the wounded iron. Everything had changed. I watched all this scornfully.

Soon the courtesy calls began. He took his pretty wife to introduce her to all the good families of the town. She was a gorgeous thing. Her eighteen years danced in her veins and glowed in her eyes. Big, black, eloquent eyes. Now I know that they were made up. Small, plump lips, a little tremulous and very

algunas monjitas que han despertado en mí un interés un poco más que casual, pero no era así entonces. Así es que yo llegué al amor un poco tarde en mi vida, y quizá por eso mi entrega fue total.

Yo la miraba con ojos de becerro en cara de cordero, y la seguía como un perro. Era un amor que no pide nada y lo da todo: la inteligencia, la voluntad y la fuerza. Amor sin mercancías, sin comercio, sin kilos de carne, sin frascos de olores, sin botellas de jugo. Sin cobros, ni cálculos, ni recibos. Amor limpio, puro, nuevo; sin manos, ni palabras, ni labios. Mudo y secreto, no va ni viene, ni siquiera está—solo es. No llega a ser idea. Es como el aire que viento impuro a ser no llega. No hay vanidad. No hay narcisismo. Es todo dulce y palpitante dolor. Un amor que es un morir—sin deseos, ni esperanzas de renacer. El amor mata—poco o mucho—y si no mata no es amor, es otra cosa. Sólo un niño es capaz del amor total.

Edumenio ya no era el mismo. Ahora era el tipo más campechano de la comarca. Risotadas, palmadas en la espalda a todo el que se le acercaba, y se le iba la boca con una facilidad espantosa. Ahora jugaba con nosotros, nos hacía de toro, o se ponía de cuatro patas para hacer de caballo. Chistes, bromas. Sus canciones, a todo poder, apagaban los aullidos y los gemidos del hierro herido. Todo había cambiado. Yo miraba todo esto con desprecio.

Pronto empezó las visitas de rigor. Llevó a presentar a su bella esposa a todas las familias decentes del pueblo. Era ella un primor. Sus dieciocho años le bailaban en las venas y le lucían en los ojos. Ojos grandes, negros, elocuentes; ahora sé que estaban pintados. Labios pequeños, gordizuelos, un poco temblorosos y muy rojos.

red. Long ear rings, showy and always quivering. She had very small feet, something that had a special attraction for me; I don't know whether it was on account of their beauty or their architecture. Everything about her was delicate and finely chiseled. Her size, her figure, her hands were the essence of femininity. She wore tight dresses and short skirts and the highest heels I had ever seen. She did not walk. Her movement was a graceful combination of the hopping of a bird and the rocking of a cradle; her rhythmic motion undulated from her smoothly rounded hips to the tips of her toes. A little pink parasol constantly moving, revolving like a whirlwind, completed the picture of a charming woman going to meet her new neighbors, incongruously hanging on the arm of a huge husband who, in contrast, seemed grotesque.

When they came to our house, we were expecting them. I was filled with an excitement that was hard to hide. I had noticed, without thinking it important, that neither my mother nor my father showed any pleasure about the imminent visit. They received the guests with exaggerated formality. I had never seen my mother so formal nor so aloof. My father came very close to being rude. The only one who did not perceive the chill in the atmosphere was Edumenio. He was proud and happy. I don't think he knew then that society was rejecting him. Having lived always on its margin, he did not know how the social apparatus operates. I am sure he thought that the formality of that afternoon was the normal thing in society. He did not realize but Henrietta did.

I was indignant. On occasions like this, people always offered refreshments. I waited and waited. Nothing happened. Finally in desperation I took the initiative that no one else was taking.

Pendientes largos, llamativos y nerviosos. Tenía chiquito el pie y esto para mí tenía atractivo especial; no sé si por su tersura o por su arquitectura. Todo en ella era delicado y fino. Tamaño, talle y manos del más puro femenino. Llevaba los vestidos ceñidos y la falda corta y los tacones más altos que yo había visto. No andaba. Su movimiento era una graciosa combinación de los saltitos de un pájaro y el mecer de una cuna, todo al compás del ritmo que bajaba hecho ondas desde sus tersas caderas hasta las puntitas de sus pies. Un pequeño parasol color de rosa en constante agitación y hecho remolino completaba la estampa de la mujer exquisita que iba a conocer a sus nuevos vecinos colgada incongruentemente del tremendo brazo de su marido que a su lado parecía grotesco.

Cuando vinieron a mi casa se les esperaba. Yo sentía una fuerte agitación que me costaba trabajo disimular. Había notado, sin darle importancia, que ni mi madre ni mi padre mostraban ningún placer en la esperada visita. Se les recibió con una exagerada formalidad. Nunca había visto yo a mi madre tan formal y remota. Mi padre andaba muy cerca de la brusquedad. El único que no parecía percatarse de la frialdad de la atmósfera era Edumenio. El se sentía orgulloso y feliz. Yo no creo que él supo entonces que la sociedad le rechazaba. Habiendo vivido siempre al margen de la sociedad él no sabía como funcionaba el aparato social. Estoy seguro que él se figuraba que la formalidad de esa tarde era lo normal en sociedad. El no se dió cuenta, pero Henriqueta sí.

Yo estaba indignado. En ocasiones como ésta se ofrecía un refrigerio. Yo esperé y esperé y como nada pasaba, en desesperación, tomé la iniciativa que nadie tomaba. "Mamá, ¿le

"Mamma, shall I tell Tocha to bring the refreshments?"

My mother was embarrassed. She stammered. Then she said, "Yes, son. Go tell her to bring us wine and cookies."

Edumenio swelled up like a toad and smiled like an idiot. At that moment, I hated him fervently.

I suppose that the reception in our house was the most civil that the bride and groom received anywhere. I heard people say that she was "one of those girls," that she was a chippy. I did not understand it then. The one thing that was sure was that the smithy again heard the shrieks of wounded iron and saw its burning tears. The smoke and soot were blacker and thicker than ever. But the smile and the song had disappeared. There was no longer either monologue or dialogue. Everything was rage and dead silence. There was no longer laughter nor jokes nor teasing—not even any bad words. What had first been a field of battle with a bronzed and noble hero standing above the smoke and the noise, what was later a place of entertainment with a clown playing the fool, had now become an inferno. Edumenio, demon-ridden, his convulsed face black with rage and strain, brandished his hammer like a weapon of vengeance, like some tool of the devil. We children fled in terror from that place.

The news soon got around. Henrietta had left Edumenio. The forge was closed. Edumenio disappeared. Years passed. The smithy went on deteriorating as all human artifacts must do. I am no longer nine years old. I am a man. But I remember and I weep. I am ashamed of human nature that denied to you, Edumenio, and to you, Henrietta, the gift of happiness that God had bestowed upon you. God proposes but man disposes.

Wherever you are, Edumenio, I hope you have another forge, where you still make war on the intractable iron. I hope that you

digo a la Tocha que traiga los refrescos?" Mi madre se cortó. Balbuceó. Luego, "sí, mi hijito, vé dile a la Tocha que nos traiga vino y bizcochitos." Edumenio se infló como un sapo y sonrió como un idiota. Lo odié fervorosamente.

Me supongo que la recepción en mi casa fue la más grata que recibieron los recién esposados. Yo oí decir que ella era una de "ésas," que era una "pluma." Yo no entendí entonces. Lo cierto es que la fragua volvió a oír los gritos de los hierros moribundos y a ver sus lágrimas encendidas. El humo y el tizne fueron más negros y espesos que nunca. Pero la sonrisa y la canción habían desaparecido. Ya no había monólogo ni diálogo. Todo era rabia y silencio. Ya no había carcajadas, ni chistes, ni bromas, ni siquiera palabrotas. Lo que primero fue campo de batalla con un héroe de bronce nobleza que se alzaba por encima del humo y del estruendo, lo que después fue sala de fiestas con un payaso haciendo el ridículo, ahora era un infierno. Edumenio, endemoniado, la cara convulsionada, negra de tensión y rabia, blandía el martillo como arma de venganza, como herramienta del diablo. Nosotros, los niños, aterrados, huimos de allí.

Pronto corrió la noticia. Henriqueta había dejado a Edumenio. Se cerró la fragua. Edumenio desapareció. Pasaron los años. La fragua se fue deshaciendo como se deshacen todas las cosas humanas. Ya no tengo nuevo años. Ya soy hombre. Pero recuerdo y lloro. Y me avergüenzo de la condición humana que les negó, a ti, Edumenio, a ti, Henriqueta, el don de la felicidad que Dios les dió. Dios manda y el hombre dispone.

Edumenio, en dondequiera que estés, espero que tengas otra fragua, y que sigas haciéndole la guerra al hierro indócil. Espero

have found your Henrietta. I hope you have a little house, clean and white, with pots of geraniums and carnations in the garden. Henrietta, I think you knew that I loved you with the purest love of my life. I hope that you have acquired—and if I could, I would give it to you—the respectability that you were seeking. I hope that in some other place among other, more generous people, you and Edumenio have forged a life full of sweetness, self-respect, and the dignity which you both deserve.

que hayas encontrado a tu Henriqueta. Espero que tengas una casita blanca y limpia con macetas de geranios y claveles en el jardín. Henriqueta, creo que supiste que yo te quise con el amor más honesto de mi vida. Espero que hayas conseguido, y si yo pudiera te la daría, la honradez que buscabas. Espero que en otro sitio, entre otras gentes más generosas, tú y Edumenio hayan fraguado una vida llena de dulzura, de amor propio y de dignidad que los dos se merecen.

MAN WITHOUT A NAME

CHAPTER I

When I finished the book that had brought me to Tierra Amarilla, my Aunt Clotilda invited all the family to celebrate. Everyone knew that I had spent the summer writing a book about my father, who had died two years before. So they already knew the subject of the work. The entire family accepted the invitation, something which amazed me. Understanding the Turriagas as I did, I knew that only a family tragedy could bring them together. I did not think my book would be a tragedy—quite the contrary—and I felt somewhat annoyed by this unexpected interest. Could it be an outpouring of family pride? It could be, for they were all dyed-in-the-wool sentimentalists. Could it be

Hombre sin nombre

CAPITULO I

Al terminar el libro que aquí me había traído, mi tía Cleotilde convidó a todos los familiares a una fiesta para celebrarlo. Todo Tierra Amarilla sabía ya que yo había pasado el verano haciendo un libro sobre mi padre fallecido hacía doce años. De modo que sabían ya de qué se trataba. Todos aceptaron la invitación, lo que me extrañó bastante. Conociendo a los Turriaga como yo los conocía, sabía que sólo una tragedia en la familia podría reunirlos. No creía yo que mi libro fuera ninguna tragedia —ni mucho menos, y me sentí irritado con este inesperado interés— ¿Sería efusión familiar? Podía serlo, porque todos eran unos sentimentales rematados. ¿Sería curiosidad morbosa? Muy

morbid curiosity? Could they want to see how I had revived the dead? Very possibly. Were they interested in my literary undertaking? Perhaps. They had always been very fond of me and had predicted a great future for me. These explanations seemed logical and reasonable, but I was still uncertain.

All my doubts were resolved by the arrival of the first guests, my Uncle Victor and Aunt Frances. When they knocked at the door, I sprang to open it. My uncle's eyes filled with tears when he saw me. He embraced me. Then I knew why they came. They were coming to my father's funeral for the second time!

This scene was repeated over and over as the guests kept arriving. The atmosphere became more and more gloomy, because the women burst into uncontrolled weeping at the arrival of each Turriaga. I felt completely discouraged and disappointed. What had been full of promise at the outset was fast changing into a memorial service.

If I had not been one hundred percent Turriaga myself, I would have ended by insulting them all. Several times I was on the point of doing so, such was my bitterness. But I knew my people. They were Turriagas first and foremost. That was their religion, a religion composed of love and hate, envy and affection, respect and scorn, nobility and vulgarity—everything good and everything bad. I looked at them with affection and forgave them once more.

Though apparently forgotten, my book lay arrogantly on the table. It was more intensely alive than any person at the gathering. It was mystery, superstition, witchcraft. It contained living specters and dead conceits. It was the splendid past of an illustrious family. They looked at it askance. Some with apprehension, others with suspicion, a few with simple curiosity,

posible. ¿Querrían ver cómo resucitaba yo a los muertos? ¿Sería interés por mi empresa literaria? Quizá. A mí me habían querido todos siempre, y siempre habían pronosticado un gran destino para mí. Estas consideraciones parecían lógicas y razonables, pero no me convencían.

Se resolvieron todas mis dudas con la llegada de los primeros huéspedes, mi tío Víctor y mi tía Francisquita. Cuando llamaron a la puerta, yo salté a abrir. En cuanto me vió mi tío se le llenaron los ojos de lágrimas y me abrazó. Entonces supe por qué venían. ¡Venían al entierro de mi padre, la segunda vez!

Esta escena se repitió muchas veces, según iban llegando los invitados. Pero aquello resultaba cada vez más triste porque las mujeres rompían a llorar desaforadamente con la llegada de cada Turriaga. Yo me sentía completamente desanimado y desilusionado. Lo que había empezado por estar lleno de promesas, se iba convirtiendo en una conmemoración fúnebre.

Si yo no hubiera sido Turriaga cien por cien habría acabado con insultarlos, y varias veces estuve al punto de hacerlo —tan amargo me sentía—. Pero yo conocía a mi gente. Primero eran Turriagas que cristianos. Esa era su religión, una religión compuesta de amor y de odio, de envidia y de cariño, de respeto y desprecio, de lo noble y lo vulgar —lo bueno y lo malo. Los contemplé con cariño y los perdoné una vez más.

Mi manuscrito yacía arrogante sobre la mesa, aparentemente olvidado. No obstante era lo más vivo de aquella concurrencia. Era el misterio, la superstición, la brujería. Contenía difuntos vivos y vanidades muertas. Era el pasado glorioso de una ilustre familia. Lo miraban de reojo. Unos con recelo, otros con sospechas, pocos con verdadera y simple curiosidad —todos con

all with real respect. What secrets might it conceal? What truths would it speak? Nobody dared mention it, and I, of course, said nothing.

My aunt passed the refreshments, a delicious chokecherry wine. This wine, whose floating lights concealed more mysteries than all the books that have been or are yet to be written, saved the occasion. It gave me my greatest triumph or my most crushing defeat. I still do not know which. In any case, the wine changed the atmosphere of the party to one of good humor and gaiety, although still obviously sentimental. Some of the family recalled the picnics we used to have in Rincón de las Nutrias, Rincón de los Apaches, and other places. Each one remembered some incident, some anecdote, some joke, some trick with which my father had charmed and delighted everyone.

The wine and the Turriaga blood had now become thoroughly mixed. Nobody realized that my father was making them laugh from beyond the grave, that the deceased was having his way with them after death as he had in life. I did. I felt his presence in a way I could not understand. It seemed to me that his spirit was emanating from my voice! Even from my own breath? I turned my thoughts inward, trying with all my being to penetrate the shadows which did not permit me to see his form even while his spirit imposed itself on my consciousness with an almost physical force.

Suddenly a voice reached me. It was Vincent, who was saying, "That Alexander! He was quite a man!" Without knowing why, I leaped proudly to my feet and shouted with a voice that even to me sounded strange. "Not just *was;* he still *is*!"

A deep silence fell like a black pall over that room full of movement and noisy chatter. Everyone looked at me, astonished

respeto—. ¿Qué secretos guardaría? ¿Qué verdades diría? Nadie se atrevía a mencionarlo, y por supuesto, yo me quedaba callado.

Mi tía pasó los refrescos, un precioso vino de capulín. Este vino, en cuyas flotantes luces había más misterios que en todos los libros escritos o por escribir, salvó la noche, me dio mi mayor triunfo o mi mayor derrota, todavía no lo sé. En todo caso el vino le dio un ambiente alegre y jocoso, aunque visiblemente sentimental, a la fiesta. Unos recordaban las romerías que antes hacíamos al Rincón de las Nutrias, al Rincón de los Apaches, y a otros sitios. Cada cual se acordaba de algún incidente, de alguna anécdota, de una broma, de un chasco con el cual mi padre había deleitado y hechizado a todo el mundo.

El vino y la sangre Turriaga se habían mezclado ya, y nadie se daba cuenta de que mi padre los estaba haciendo reír desde ultratumba, de que el difunto andaba haciendo de las suyas entre ellos después de la muerte como antes lo había hecho en la vida. Yo sí. Yo sentía su presencia de una manera que no me podía explicar. ¡Me parecía que su espíritu estaba emanando de mi voz! ¿De mi propio aliento? Me perdí en mí mismo tratando con todo mi ser de penetrar las nieblas que no me permitían ver su figura cuando su alma se imprimía en mi sensibilidad con una fuerza casi física.

De repente una voz llegó a mi conciencia. Era Vicente que decía: "Ese Alejandro sí que era un hombre." Sin saber por qué, yo me puse de pie soberbiamente y le grité, con una voz que a mí mismo me pareció extraña: "¡No lo era; todavía lo es!"

Un silencio profundo cayó como un manto negro sobre la sala llena de agitación y algazara. Todo el mundo me miraba con

and fearful. When I realized what I had done, I did not know where to turn. I stammered something to the effect that as long as a Turriaga could laugh, Alexander would still live. There were some nervous titters here and there, and the conversation was resumed.

When the celebration had reached its height, Uncle Victor asked for the floor and began to speak. I swelled with pride, hearing again that sonorous, rich, and impassioned voice that had always impressed me when I was young. I remembered the political campaigns in which Uncle Victor had made his audience laugh or cry while I listened enraptured and swore that some day I would be an orator like him. Now his voice vibrated with emotion as he spoke of my sacrifices and my triumphs.

"And now," he concluded, "I am going to ask my nephew to tell us about his book. That's why we are here."

Tremulous with emotion, I stood up and looked at those wild and passionate people of mine. I had never loved my family as I did at that moment when its members watched me silently, a thousand questions in their eyes. I felt that my poor book stood before the severest possible tribunal—that if this court accepted it, it had achieved success. But if there was a false note in it, it would be dashed to failure here, this very night. Alexander had been the idol, the personification, and the spiritual leader of the Turriagas. They would not permit me, nor would I want, to sell him short.

Conscious of all this, my thoughts turbulent and fearful, I began to speak. I told them how I had promised my mother that I would construct a monument to my father, and that this book was that monument. Little by little, I lost myself in the story. My listeners hung on my words, even snatching them from my lips, as we lived

espanto y miedo. Yo, cuando me di cuenta de lo que había hecho, no sabía qué hacer. Balbucí algo sobre el hecho de que mientras un Turriaga pudiera reír, viviría Alejandro. Hubo unas risitas nerviosas aquí y ahí y se reanudó la conversación.

Cuando la fiesta alcanzó su apogeo, mi tío Víctor pidió la palabra y empezó a hablar. Me llené de orgullo al oír una vez más su voz sonora, rotunda y apasionada que siempre me había impresionado cuando yo era joven. Recordé las campañas políticas en las que Victoriano hacía llorar o reír a su auditorio mientras yo le escuchaba embobado y juraba que algún día sería yo un orador como él. Ahora la voz le vibraba con emoción hablando de mis sacrificios y mis triunfos. "Y ahora, terminó, le voy a pedir a mi sobrino que nos diga de su libro, a eso hemos venido."

Trémulo de emocíon, me puse de pie y contemplé a aquella gente mía, apasionada y bárbara, que jamás había querido como la quise en aquel momento, y que me miraba silenciosamente con mil interrogaciones en los ojos. Sentí en ese momento que mi pobre libro estaba ante el tribunal más severo y que si éste lo aceptaba, quedaría logrado. Pero si había una nota falsa en él, aquí fracasaría aquella misma noche. Alejandro había sido el ídolo, la personificación y el jefe espiritual de los Turriaga, y ellos no me permitirían, y yo no querría, perjudicarlo.

Consciente de todo esto y con el alma alborotada y medrosa me puse a hablar. Les conté cómo le había prometido a mi madre levantarle un monumento a mi padre. y que este mi libro era el monumento. Poco a poco me fui perdiendo en mi relato. Mis oyentes estaban pendientes de cada una de mis palabras, me las

the past together. Even when they began to realize the direction in which the theme was veering—the mental and spiritual struggle of an Alexander whom they never knew—even then they gave me their earnest attention. I saw in their eyes the effort to understand, the question whether to believe or disbelieve. One by one they were becoming convinced of the significance of incidents they had attributed to "Alexander's way" without stopping to evaluate them. They began to perceive the reality behind outward appearances. Their faces revealed the surprise with which they received an Alexander who had lived and died among them without their really knowing him. But they recognized him as legitimate. I am sure of that. I read in their eyes that they loved him as they had loved the other, that the reality of my Alexander was as authentic as theirs, perhaps more so.

I was so absorbed in my own feelings at the end of my talk that I did not realize the uneasy silence that had descended upon the group. They were astonished. They were bewildered, disoriented, as a result of my revelations. I had snatched them out of their world, and they could find no way to get back to it. Their spirits struggled with incomprehensible things in an alien region where I had evoked a figure at once familiar and unknown. They struggled back to the threatened security of familiar things at last, heartsore and fearful. Their eyes, big with questions, watched me with something akin to fright.

Gumersindo, badly disturbed, suggested a toast to the new author in the family. Excessive applause followed this suggestion, as if each one sought in noise and physical action a way to regain the serenity that he had lost. We all drank eagerly, for we needed a drink badly. Everyone congratulated me.

quitaban a veces al salir de la boca, y vivíamos todos juntos el pasado. Aun cuando empezaron a darse cuenta del rumbo al que iba virando el tema —la lucha mental y espiritual que fue la vida de un Alejandro que ellos nunca conocieron —aun entonces me siguieron prestando su atención. Yo veía en sus ojos el esfuerzo por comprender, la duda entre el creer y el no creer. Uno por uno se fueron convenciendo del verdadero significado e importancia de incidentes que ellos habían atribuído a las "cosas de Alejandro" sin detenerse a valorarlas. Empezaron a percibir la realidad detrás de las apariencias. Sus caras revelaban la sorpresa con que iban recibiendo a un Alejandro que vivió y murió sin que ellos lo conocieran. Pero lo reconocieron como legítimo. Estoy seguro. Leí en sus miradas que lo querían como habían querido al otro, que la realidad de mi Alejandro era tan auténtica como la que ellos le habían dado al suyo, y quizá más. Su vida y su muerte quedaban justificadas.

Quedé tan ensimismado al final de la lectura que ni me di cuenta del silencio inquietante que había descendido sobre el grupo. Estaban asombrados. Estaban aturdidos, fuera de quicio, con mis revelaciones. Los había sacado de su mundo y no podían regresar a él. Su espíritu luchaba con lo incomprensible del más allá en el que yo había evocado una figura al mismo tiempo familiar y desconocida, y por fin regresaban a la seguridad, ya amenazada, de lo conocido, abatidos y medrosos. Sus ojos preguntones me miraban con algo parecido al espanto.

Gumersindo, todo descompuesto, sugirió un brindis al nuevo autor de la familia. El aplauso que acompañó a esta sugestión fue excesivo, como si cada cual buscara en la acción física y en el ruido la manera de recuperar el sosiego que había perdido. De

Finally my turn came to propose a toast. I was now quite gay, and my earlier apprehensions had begun to disappear. I took the glass of wine, raised it with a Turriagaesque gesture, and exclaimed, "Let us drink to the monument to my father, to the monument erected in those pages with love, respect, and admiration. Let us drink his favorite toast. You remember how he used to look at himself in his glass and say, 'Let each one drink to himself, and thus he will live forever.' " And taking the glass in both hands, as I had seen my father do so many times, I looked at myself in the wine.

My God! I should never have done it! It was not my face that undulated and smiled in the trembling wine of my cup. The face in that bloody mirror was that of my dead father!

Death was looking at me. It was not the sombre death that I had witnessed on the battlefield, but an amiable and familiar death that looked out at me through my father's face. Desperately, I drank the toast and collapsed on a chair, almost unconscious. The watching guests were frightened for a moment. Then, thinking me only overcome by emotion, they drank and applauded me noisily.

Little by little I recovered myself and a few moments later I was laughing and joking with the rest. I had never been—as I now think—so amusing and so charming as that night. Everything I said had a jocose tone, and my gaiety floated contagiously through the room provoking, tempting, seducing, titillating. It was as if it were not mine. It was as if I were no longer I.

Some of them realized it.

"A chip off the old block," someone said.

"Like father, like son," another added.

"Alexander would have said, 'Son of a so-and-so,' " remarked a third.

muy buena gana bebimos todos, que bien lo necesitábamos. Todo el mundo me felicitaba.

Al fin me tocó brindar a mí. Ya me encontraba bastante alegre y mis aprensiones anteriores se empezaban a disipar. Tomé la copa de vino y la levanté con un gesto muy turriaguesco y exclamé: "Bebamos al monumento de mi padre, al monumento que amasé en estas páginas con cariño, respeto y admiración. Bebamos pues, al brindis favorito de mi padre, que mirándose en su copa de vino solía decir: "Bebámonos cada *quien* a sí mismo, y así viviremos para siempre." Y tomando la copa con las dos manos, como tantas veces había visto hacer a mi padre, me miré en el vino.

¡Nunca lo hubiera hecho, Dios mío! La cara que ondulaba y sonreía en el trémulo vino de mi copa no era la mía. ¡La cara en el espejo sanguíneo de mi copa era la de mi difunto podre!

La muerte me estaba mirando. No era la muerte tenebrosa que presentí en los campos de batalla. Era una muerte afable y familiar que me miraba a través de la cara de mi padre. Me la bebí desesperadamente y me desplomé sobre un sillón casi sin sentido. Me miraron asustados por un momento, pero luego, creyéndome solamente dominado por la emoción, bebieron y me aplaudieron tumultuosamente.

Fui recobrando el brío poco a poco y momentos después reía y disparataba con los demás. Nunca había sido yo —según pienso ahora— tan gracioso y simpático como esa noche. Todo lo que decía tenía un eco de algazara y mi alegría flotaba contagiosa por la habitación provocando, tentando, seduciendo con su cosquilleo. Era como si no fuera mía. Era como si yo no fuera yo.

Hubo quien se dio cuenta. "De tal palo, tal astilla," dijo alguien. "De tales padres, tales hijos," añadió otro. "Alejandro hubiera dicho, "hijos de un tal . . ." agregó el tercero. Y las

The women put the idea in more concrete terms.

"Look at him, Florentina!" said an aunt. "Why, he is exactly like my brother, the spitting image of him!"

"Yes. Even that crease between his eyes is the same as Alexander had."

I heard all this happily.

There was, however, a false note in that hilarity. When I had to go out at night as a child, I started whistling so that nobody would know I was afraid—and also to deceive myself. That was exactly what was happening that night in my aunt's house. They were all laughing and singing to hide the fear they were denying. They were denying it as I denied the existence of the witches and goblins I feared in my childhood, as atheists deny the existence of God.

Gradually an indefinable horror, which I tried to hide, began to penetrate my mind. I wanted to be alone to struggle with my mystery, to analyze the strange anguish that gripped me, to examine the extraordinary experience that I had undergone. I felt that I must think it all over rationally. Finally I saw with relief that the guests were getting ready to leave.

But the strangest experience still awaited me. When they said good-bye to me, when their puzzled eyes looked into my face, when they gave me a trembling handshake and slipped away into the street, they were acting as if it had been the deceased Alexander who had amused and entertained them that night. They had decided that I was no longer I! That I was my father!

mujeres, concretando más, decían: "Míralo, Florentina, si es uno mismo con mi hermano, alma mía de él." "Sí, respondía mi tía, hasta esa arruga que tiene entre los ojos es la que tenía Alejandro." Yo oía todo esto feliz.

Había en aquella hilaridad una nota falsa. Cuando yo era niño y tenía que salir de noche, me ponía a silbar para que nadie supiera que tenía miedo, y también para engañarme a mí mismo. Eso era precisamente lo que pasaba allí aquella noche. Reían y cantaban para ocultar el miedo que ellos mismos se negaban. Se lo negaban como yo de niño negaba la existencia de brujas y aparecidos, temiéndolos, como los ateos niegan la existencia de Dios.

A mí mismo me empezó a entrar un terror indefinible que traté de ocultar. Quería estar solo para luchar con mi misterio, para analizar las extrañas sensaciones y congojas que sentía, para investigar las raras experiencias que sufrí, someterlo todo a la prueba de la razón. Vi con alivio que las visitas se preparaban a marcharse.

Pero me faltaba la experiencia más extraña. Al despedirse de mí, al mirarme, confusos, a los ojos, al darme la mano temblorosa, al salir evasivos a la calle, lo hacían como si fuera el difunto Alejandro quien los había divertido y festejado aquella noche. ¡Decidieron que yo ya no era yo! ¡Que yo era mi padre!

CHAPTER II

I went up to my room in despair, stumbling at every step, and threw myself upon the bed. I saw nothing, heard nothing. I felt only a dull, leaden pain between my eyes, a buzzing in my ears. My heart pounded as if trying to beat its way out of my breast. My intestines were contracted into hard knots. I thought I must be dying or going crazy. I could not think. I could not weep.

Suddenly a dry, harsh sob, the kind that burns and leaves permanent scars on the soul, surged from the profoundest depths of my being and exploded in the vacuum of my consciousness. Another followed it and another. That violent weeping, mute as the tomb, dry as musty death, burning as the flames of hell, shook and consumed me. There in the fire, in the noise, in the convulsion, in the chaos of my universe, my two worlds, the conscious and the subconscious, crashed into one another, and careened away from their natural orbits. I died and was born again. And I did not know it.

Overborne and trembling, I lay on the bed, without will, without resistance, abjectly suspended between the here and the beyond. My wide-stretched eyes stared into space without seeing, but waiting. My ears crackled. They heard nothing, but they were listening. My heart kept on beating because it did not know how to stop, but it was preparing itself. In short, all my being—or whatever I now was—was waiting avidly and fearfully, in a state of suspended animation, for the hand and voice of God to give it abilities and direction. It was as if I were another Lazarus, dead but conscious, awaiting the voice of someone who would say, "Arise and walk."

Into this dense silence fell a familiar but long-forgotten voice.

CAPITULO II

Subí a mi habitación desesperado, tropezando con todo, y me eché sobre la cama. No veía nada, ni oía nada. Sólo sentía un dolor sordo y pesado entre los ojos y tenía un zumbido en los oídos. El corazón quería salírseme. Tenía las tripas contraidas en nudos duros. Sentí que me moría o me hacía loco. No podía pensar. No podía llorar.

De pronto un sollozo, árido y áspero, de esos que queman y dejan cicatrices permanentes en el alma, nació en lo más profundo de mi ser y estalló en el vacío de mi conciencia. Lo siguió otro, y otro, y aquel violento llanto, mudo como la tumba, seco como la muerte, abrazador como el infierno, me estremecía y me consumía. Ahí en el fuego, en el estruendo, en las erupciones, en el caos de mi universo mis dos mundos, mi conciencia y mi inconsciencia, se chocaron, andando ambos fuera de sus órbitas. Me morí y volví a nacer. Y no lo supe.

Quedé vencido y trémulo sobre la cama, sin voluntad, sin resistencia, suspendido abyectamente entre el aquí y el más allá. Los ojos abiertos grandes, fijos en el espacio, sin ver, pero esperando. Mis oídos chisporroteaban; no oían pero escuchaban. Mi corazón seguía latiendo porque no sabía cómo parar; pero se preparaba. En fin todo mi ser, o lo que ahora era, esperaba, anhelante y medroso, en una especie de animación suspendida, la mano y la voz de Dios que le diera sus facultades y su destino. Era como si yo fuera un Lázaro, muerto pero consciente, esperando la voz de alguien que le dijera, "Levántate y anda."

En este silencio denso cayó una voz conocida y olvidada. ¡La

The voice of my father! The shocked terror I felt when I first heard and then understood his words is indescribable. Confused, overcome, horrified, I exclaimed,

"I do not know whether I am really hearing nor whether I understand. I do not even know who you are. By the love of my mother, set me free from this torturing uncertainty."

"Calm down, Alex, and listen to me. You should not be surprised that I am here, for you have been suspecting my presence for a long time."

"But where do you come from?"

"From many places, son, but mostly from you yourself."

"What do you mean—from me?"

"Exactly that. A part of my being has lived all these years, hidden and forgotten, in you."

"But why did you wait until now? Why have you come to pursue me?"

"You are wrong, my son. I did not come to pursue you; you came looking for me. I was only awaiting your arrival."

"You confuse me. I did not come in search of you. I don't even admit that you exist, nor that this is anything more than a dream."

"If life is a dream, then this is a dream; if not, this is reality. Believe me, Alex, if I exist—and I do because you have given me a second existence—you have recreated me. The mere fact that you are talking with me proves my reality. You grant me personality by listening to me."

I sat up in bed, terrified. The full import of what was happening had penetrated my mind. I began to understand the danger I was in, and my entire being organized itself, bodily and mentally, for defense. I suddenly realized that the worst had happened, that the greatest threat I had faced in my entire life was before me. I was

voz de mi padre! Mi sobresalto al oír primero, y comprender mucho después sus palabras es inexplicable. Todo confuso, vencido y horrorizado, exclamé:

—No sé si oigo, ni si entiendo, ni siquiera quién eres. ¡Por el amor de mi madre, sácame de esta duda!

—Sosiégate, Alejandrito, y escúchame. El que yo esté aquí no te sorprende tanto porque ya hace tiempo te lo vienes sospechando.

—¿Pero de dónde vienes?

—De muchas partes, hijo, pero principalmente de tí mismo.

—¿Cómo de mí mismo?

—Precisamente eso. Parte de mi ser ha vivido todos estos años oculto y olvidado en tí.

—¿Y por qué te aguardaste hasta ahora? ¿Por qué vienes a perseguirme?

—Te equivocas hijo. Yo no vine a perseguirte a tí; tú viniste en pos de mí. Yo sólo esperaba tu venida.

—Me confundes. Yo no vine ni fui por tí. Ni aun admito que eres, ni que esto es nada más que un sueño.

—Si la vida es sueño, esto es sueño, si no, esto es verdad. Créemelo, Alejandrito, sí existo, y existo porque tú me has dado existencia otra vez, me has vuelto a crear. El mero hecho que hablas conmigo comprueba mi realidad. Tú me concedes personalidad escuchándome.

Me senté en la cama asustado. Al fin había penetrado en mi entendimiento lo que me estaba pasando. Empecé a enterarme del peligro en que me hallaba, y todo mi ser se organizó, corporal y mentalmente, para la defensa. Supe de pronto que las cosas no podían estar peores, que ante mí estaba la mayor amenaza de mi

about to lose my mind, my personality, my very being. I understood that if I lost this struggle, I would no longer be what I had been, what others thought me to be. I would die. I had to defend myself!

A peal of laughter, resonant, gay, somewhat mocking, cut abruptly into my anxiety. It was my father. Yes, it was he. I no longer had the slightest doubt. But my determination not to surrender grew stronger and stronger.

"Don't forget, my boy, that you cannot hide anything from me—as you never could. Living inside you, I know your most intimate thoughts." There was triumph in his voice, mixed with a tinge of something like compassion that did nothing to reassure me.

"Very well, Father." I answered, trying to hide my terror. "For the time being, I accept your existence, if that is what it is. But I warn you that I will tear you out of my consciousness at the first opportunity. You lived your life; let me live mine."

"You no longer have the power to take away my life. You had the power to resuscitate me or not, as you pleased. But once having done so, you will have to put up with me as long as you live, because I shall live, even after you. But let us suppose that you could plunge me back into the oblivion from which you brought me, don't you think it would be cruel to do so?"

"I was able to give you life, and I can take it away. And don't talk to me about cruelty when you are planning to kill me. I held your memory in love and respect, and now you want to repay me by destroying me completely. I have to take away that life I accidentally gave you in order to continue my own existence. A man must kill in order to live."

"You have certainly developed a frightful selfishness in my

vida. Estaba para perder la mente, la personalidad, o el mismo ser. Supe que si perdía esta lucha dejaría de ser lo que era, lo que otros creían que era, moriría. ¡Tendría que defenderme!

Una carcajada sonora, alegre y algo burlona, cortó mis cavilaciones abruptamente. Era mi padre. Sí, sí era. Ya no me cabía duda. Pero mi determinación de no rendirme se hacía cada vez más fuerte.

—No olvides, hijo mío, que no me puedes ocultar nada, como nunca pudiste, que viviendo dentro de tí conozco tus más íntimos pensamientos. Había triunfo en su voz mezclado con cierta compasión que no convencía.

—Muy bien padre, le respondí, queriendo ocultar mi terror, acepto por ahora tu realidad, si es que la tienes. Pero te advierto que te arrancaré de mí conciencia a la prímera oportunidad. Tú viviste tu vida; déjame vivir la mía.

—No puedes ya quitarme la vida. Pudiste resucitarme o no. Habiéndome resucitado, tendrás que aguantarme mientras vivas, porque aun después de tí viveré. Pero supongamos que pudieras hundirme en el olvido de donde me sacaste, ¿no te parece cruel matarme?

—Como pude darte la vida sabré quitártela. Y no me hables de crueldad siendo que tú te propones quitarme la vida a mí. Yo mantuve tu memoria con amor y respeto y tú me quieres pagar con aniquilarme. Tengo que quitarte la vida prestada y accidental que te di para poder vivir yo. Para vivir hay que matar.

—Has desarrollado un egoísmo espantoso durante mi ausencia.

absence. What would you say if I told you that you are the one who does not exist—that you never did exist?"

"I would say that you are crazy, that you died a long time ago. How would you explain my personality, which is completely different from yours?"

"Look here, Alex. Listen to me carefully. The personality and the inner being are two different things. I admit that your personality is your own. You forged it little by little, but the interior materials you used were mine. With them, through your experiences and contacts with outside reality, your personality was formed. You were its architect. Personality, nevertheless, is an exterior thing. But your inner being was always mine. When you were born, you had no character, and I imposed mine upon you before you could develop your own. It was no accident that I gave you the name you bear, that I indoctrinated you in your impressionable years, showed you my soul and wrapped you in it, taught you my songs, gave you my desires, my faults, my anxieties, my hatreds. In short, from your baby days I absorbed you and lived in you. Think carefully, and you will remember that I conditioned every idea, thought, and act that formed your ego—in my own image—and I was there within that image."

There was so much truth in what he said, his logic was so unassailable, that I felt myself weakening again. I looked into my own heart and saw in the gloom of my universe shadowy masses of forgotten things that were beginning to stretch and shake off their long sleep. Terrified, I saw them form in line and march one by one toward the light of consciousness to present themselves for recognition. I knew many of them, but among them were things I had not forgotten and others that were not mine to forget. It was a conspiracy of dead things no longer dead, that, like my father, had

¿Qué dirías si yo te dijera que eres tú el que no existe, y que nunca exististe?

—Diría que estás loco, que tú dejaste de existir ya hace mucho. ¿Cómo explicas mi personalidad que es completamente distinta a la tuya?

—Mira, Alejandrito, esúchame bien. La personalidad y el ser son dos cosas distintas. Admito que tu personalidad es toda tuya. Tú te la has forjado poco a poco, pero los materiales interiores de los cuales te valiste eran míos. Con ellos, a través de tus experiencias y contactos con la realidad exterior, se fue formando tu personalidad, por lo tanto, es cosa exterior. Más tu íntimo ser fue mío siempre. Cuando tú naciste no tenías ser ninguno, y yo te impuse el mío antes que tuvieras uno propio. Con segunda intención te di el nombre que llevas, te indoctriné en tus años impresionantes, te mostré mi alma y te envolví en ella, te enseñé mis canciones, te di mis apetitos, mis pecados, mis penas, mis odios. En fin, desde tu edad más tierna, yo te absorbí, y viví en tí. Piensa bien y recuerda que yo condicioné todas las ideas, pensamientos, y hechos que formaron tu ser —en mi propia imagen— y dentro de esta imagen estaba yo.

Había tanto de verdad en lo que él decía, su lógica era tan inquebrantable que me sentí flaquear otra vez. Me asomé en mi alma y vi en la niebla de mi universo los bultos de mis olvidos que empezaban a desperezarse y a sacudirse de su largo sueño. Los vi con temor hacerse fila y marchar uno por uno hacia la luz de la conciencia y darse a conocer. Conocí muchos, pero entre ellos había olvidos que yo no había olvidado. Era una conjuración de difuntos, que ya no eran difuntos, que como mi padre habían vuelto de entre los muertos a torturarme, a hacer partido con él

come back from the tomb to torture me, to side with him against me. Among my own memories, there were many also that supported my father. How galling to be betrayed four times! By my own memories, by memories disguised as mine, by my forgotten experiences, and by forgotten experiences that I had never had but that presented themselves as mine. It was a formidable force that could destroy me.

And what resources could I count on? I saw with relief that thousands of legitimate memories of my own intellectual, emotional, and physical experiences were forming in opposition to the traitors. Allied with them were my loyal forgotten experiences, now wearing the uniform of memory. And from all sides, marching with great dignity, came squads of ambitions, of dreams, of desires. These were mine. These were loyal. Forming all these diverse forces into a martial column came the general of my universe, my will. His manner was resolute. A smile of confidence was on his face. As long as he did not weaken, everything would come out all right.

I saw all this in the shadowy depths of my soul. I saw the masses among the masses, the shadows among the shadows. I heard echoes of laughter, moans, and sobbing long dead. I saw, I listened, and I regained my courage. Hope returned—elusive and diffident at first, bold and aggressive later on. I felt life, hot, wet, electrifying, surge once more through my veins, and this reaction of my own flesh began to actuate my confidence in myself. I faced my father and took the initiative.

"You know, Father, I am getting over my fear because I am beginning to understand you. I am discovering your strengths and your weaknesses. Your power is in me, and your weakness is in yourself. I can make use of both to overcome you. Don't try to

contra mí. Entre mis recuerdos había tantos que también soportaban a mi padre. ¡Qué feo es ser traicionado cuatro veces! Por mis recuerdos; por los recuerdos que no eran míos, disfrazados como míos; por mi olvidos; y por olvidos ajenos que llevaban mi marca. Era un fuerza formidable que me podía destruir.

¿Y con qué recursos podía contar yo? Vi con alivio que opuestos a los traidores se iban formando millares de mis recuerdos legítimos de mis experiencias intelectuales, emocionales, y físicas. Aliados con ellos estaban mis olvidos leales, ya vestidos con el uniforme de la memoria. Y de todos rumbos venían marchando con suma dignidad patrullas de ambiciones, de ensueños, de deseos; éstos eran míos; éstos eran leales. Aliñando todas estas diversas fuerzas en línea marcial andaba el general de mi universo, mi voluntad, su manera resuelta, en su cara una sonrisa de confianza. Mientras ella no flaqueara, todo saldría bien.

Todo esto vi en el claroscuro de mi alma. Vi los bultos entre los bultos y las sombras entre las sombras. Oí los ecos de risas, de gemidos, de llantos, ya muertos. Vi, escuché, y recobré ánimo. Volvieron mis esperanzas —esquivas y hurañas primero, amantes y agresivas después—. Sentí la vida, caliente, húmeda, y electrificante correr en mis venas una vez más, y con esta sensualidad empezó a actuar mi confianza en mí mismo. Me encaré con mi padre y le tomé la iniciativa.

—Sabes, papá, que ya te voy perdiendo el miedo, porque ya te empiezo a comprender. Ya voy conociendo tus fuerzas y tus flaquezas. Tu poder está en mí y tu debilidad está en tí. Sabré valerme de ambos para vencerte. No trates de embaucarme. Somos

trick me. We are mortal enemies. One of us must die, and I have no intention of letting myself get killed."

"I am glad that you understand me, but that business of our being mortal enemies is ridiculous. You always liked to dramatize yourself. If you understand me, you will love me, because knowing people means loving them. There is no reason why, knowing one another and respecting one another, we cannot live together. You can't even conceive of what a tremendous thing it would be for you. Imagine the intellectual force that would be yours if you had recourse to two minds, two lives, to intellectual dimensions never before known to man—the present, the past, the future, and the beyond. My experiences and my unprecedented knowledge would be of incalculable value to you. I could make you the most illustrious man in the world."

"That idea of living together in one body is pure self-delusion. One or the other must die, unless one lives completely subjugated to the will of the other. The first would be preferable. I admit that what you propose might be possible, that I or you or both of us might come to be the most outstanding man that has ever lived. But at the same time, he would be the most unfortunate, tormented man that hell could produce. In any case, I refuse your offer. I will be what I can be through my own efforts. So I beg you, by the love you once had for me—if it was not solely self-love—by the love of my mother, by the love I had for you, to return to the repose in which I found you and leave me in my former peace. If you do that, I will always love and venerate you, and you will live in even greater esteem in my memory for having sacrificed yourself that I might live. If you don't do it, I can't help hating you and I will have to kill you. The only thing that will be left of you will be a bitter, stinking memory which I will do my best to

enemigos mortales; uno de nosotros ha de morir, y yo no tengo ningunas intenciones de dejarme matar.

—Me alegra eso de que me comprendas, pero eso de que somos enemigos mortales es una insensatez. Siempre te gustó dramatizarte. Si me comprendes, me querrás porque el conocer es querer. No hay por qué conociéndonos y estimándonos no podamos vivir juntos. Para tí sería una realización tan tremenda que ni te la puedes figurar. Imagínate la fuerza intelectual que sería tuya si te valías de dos intelectos, de dos vidas, de dimensiones intelectuales jamás conocidas entre los hombres: el presente, el pasado, el futuro, el más allá. Mis experiencias y conocimientos inauditos te serían de inefable valor. Yo podría hacer de tí el más insigne de los hombres.

—Eso de vivir juntos en una persona es pura quimera. Uno u otro tiene que morir, a no ser que uno viva subyugado a la voluntad del otro. En este caso, lo primero sería preferible. Admito que lo que tú propones sea posible, que yo, o tú, o los dos, llegaría a ser el hombre más notable que jamás ha habido, pero a la vez sería el hombre más desgraciado y torturado que el infierno ha producido. En todo caso, rehuso tu oferta. Llegaré a ser lo que fuere por mi propia cuenta. De modo que te pido que por el amor que me tuviste, si no fue amor propio, por el amor de mi madre, por lo que yo te he querido, que regreses al reposo en que te hallé y me dejes a mí en el que me encontraste. Si así lo hicieres te querré y te veneraré y vivirás en mi memoria aun en mayor estimación por haberte sacrificado para que yo viviera. Si no lo haces, no puedo menos que odiarte y tendré que matarte, y lo único que quedará de tí será una memoria rencorosa y fétida que haré lo posible por erradicar. Si sigo recordándote, será sólo para

eliminate. Are you going as a kindly spirit, or will you stay as an evil spirit?"

"You defend yourself like a man. You are my son. I know your problem even better than you, for I see farther in all directions, above and below things. But I cannot do what you want, nor am I able to feel any pity for you. Even if I wanted to, I cannot commit suicide because I am a spirit, and I have no way to do so. In order for me to die, you would have to die, too, for I live only in you. I cannot pity you, for I do not have the necessary equipment. For tears, compassion and love, one has to have eyes, a heart, a body. As long as you deny me yours—and I cannot penetrate into them as I have into your spirit—I am incapable of any emotion. No, Alex. Don't struggle against me. Resign yourself and let's be friends. Let's conquer the world together."

The night passed in these and other arguments. At times my spirit soared to the heights of optimism, only to plummet later into the most dismal pessimism. Then I would begin to rise again like a wounded but indomitable eagle. Meanwhile, I began to perceive that, if my spirit was weakened, that of my adversary was failing even more. Even his voice died away. In one of those instants that seem like an eternity, I saw my salvation for the first time. If my father's spirit was faltering, it was because he lacked strength, strength that I alone could give him or deny him. It was true that I had gone many places stirring and collecting particles of his being in order to create the phantom that was threatening me. But many particles were lacking. The aggregation of the rest was still defective. My task was to avoid the discovery of the missing ones and cause the disintegration of those collected before their cohesion was complete.

This ray of hope thawed the ice of my tears, which had numbed

maldecirte. ¿Te vas como un espírtu bueno o te quedas como un espíritu malo?

—Te defiendes como un hombre. Eres hijo mío. Conozco tu problema aún mejor que tú porque veo más allá y más acá que tú, por arriba y por debajo de las cosas, pero no puedo hacer lo que me pides, ni puedo compadecerme de tí. Aunque quisiera, no puedo suicidarme porque soy espíritu y me faltan los medios. Para que yo muera tendrás que morir tú también porque sólo vivo en tí. No me compadezco de tí porque también me falta lo necesario. Para las lágrimas, la compasión, y el amor, es necesario tener ojos, corazón, y estómago. Mientras tú me niegues los tuyos, y yo no pueda penetrar en ellos como penetré en tu alma, yo soy incapaz de toda emoción. No Alejandrito, no luches contra mí. Resígnate y vamos siendo amigos, vamos conquistando esos mundos.

En esto y otros argumentos se fue la noche. Mi espíritu subía a ratos al más alto optimismo para dar después contra el suelo del pesimismo más lamentable. Luego volvía a subir, cual águila herida pero indomable. Entre tanto empecé a percibir que si mi espíritu se encontraba debilitado, el de mi adversario iba falleciendo aun más. Hasta que su voz se apagó. En uno de esos instantes que son una eternidad vi mi salvación por la primera vez. Si el espíritu de mi padre se desmayaba era porque le faltaban fuerzas, fuerzas que sólo yo podía darle o negarle. Era verdad que yo había recorrido mucha tierra removiendo y recogiendo átomos de su ser, congregándolos para reconstruir el fantasma que me amenazaba. Pero había todavía muchos átomos que le hacían falta. La agregación de los demás era todavía defectuosa. Mi tarea era evitar el descubrimiento de aquéllos y causar la disgregación de éstos antes de su cementación.

Este rayo de esperanza deshizo el hielo de mis lágrimas, que me

my brain. And I wept. I wept. I wept as I had not done since the disappointments of childhood. I wept senselessly, abandoned by my intellect which was lying, overcome with exhaustion, near its adversary, another intellect, equally exhausted. I wept and bathed that spirit of mine that had defended me so nobly, bathed it with tears that I had saved for that moment through an entire lifetime. I stopped weeping only when the last tear evaporated in the fever of my soul.

Then I began to walk up and down the room, from one side to the other. I tried to think. I could not. I kept on walking. I tried to pray. The prayers that I knew did not suit the occasion. The ones I formulated sounded false to me. I remembered to smoke. I smoked. I walked and smoked, but I could not think. Suddenly I found myself at the window and looked out, without knowing what I was doing.

It was that magic moment of early dawn when it is neither day nor night. I saw the masses of the shadows and the shadows of the masses detaching themselves and melting again into the blackness. I heard the cries of animals or of desire. Perhaps sobs. I do not know. I heard and saw all this. And I did not know whether I was observing the dawn or my own heart. I fell asleep, or I fainted. I do not know. And I dreamed two dreams, one pleasant, one a nightmare.

CHAPTER III

I went down to breakfast very late. My uncle had already gone to work. It was a lovely day, as autumn days are in Tierra

tenía el cerebro entumido. Y lloré. Lloré. Lloré como no había llorado desde las primeras desilusiones de mi niñez. Lloré sin sentido, abandonado por el intelecto que yacía vencido junto a otro intelecto vencido, adversario suyo. Lloré y bañé a este espíritu mío que tan noblemente me había defendido, lo bañé con las lágrimas que había guardado toda una vida para este momento. Dejé de llorar cuando la última lágrima se evaporó en al calentura de mi alma.

Después empecé a pasearme de una orilla del aposento al otro. Quise pensar. No pude. Seguí andando. Quise rezar. Las oraciones que sabía no daban al caso. Las que formulé me sonaron falsas. Me acordé de fumar. Fumé. Anduve y fumé pero no pude pensar. De pronto me encontré en la ventana y me asomé para fuera. Sin saber que me asomaba. Sin saber que no me asomaba.

Era ese momento mágico de la madrugada cuando la noche y el día se disputan la supremacía. Vi los bultos de las sombras y las sombras de los bultos despegándose y volviéndose a pegar a la negrura. Oí cantos de animales o de deseos. Tal vez llantos. No sé. Todo vesto vi y oí. Y no supe si contemplaba el alba o mi alma misma. Y me dormí, o me desmayé. No sé. Y soñé dos sueños. Uno bueno. Uno malo.

CAPITULO III

Ya era tarde cuando bajé al desayuno. Ya mi tío se había ido a trabajar. Era un día precioso como son los días de otoño en Tierra

Amarilla. There was in the air a subtle invitation to relaxation and dreaming, but flying above and mixed with this tranquility, fleeting, mysterious gusts wafted the threat of frost that would soon be there. Something of dreams, something of death.

My aunt, busy with her chores, was so distracted that she did not hear me come in. When I greeted her, she jumped and uttered a stifled cry, looking at me as if she were frightened. She controlled herself immediately and said, "I did not wake you, son, because I thought you must be tired and would need the rest."

She did not ask me the customary question about how I had slept, from which fact I deduced that last night's happenings had not escaped her. But I did not want to discuss the matter, either. Particularly when I noticed that she kept watching me out of the corner of her eye and that she was maintaining her distance.

I ate breakfast eagerly. For days, I had not had the appetite I had that morning, and I was delighted with the country breakfast she gave me: eggs, roasted ribs, fried potatoes, gravy, toast, and cheese baked with sugar. I ate a great deal. It seemed that, by eating, I was trying to fill an inner emptiness—or hide something hideous. Apparently the body defends itself from death when the spirit fails. I kept eating, and my aunt watched me in silence.

We did not talk. We had nothing to say to one another, or rather, we could not or did not want to say what was in our minds. Breakfast over, I went out into the street. I found myself deeply depressed, without energy, without spirit. I tried to think about last night, but thought in concrete form escaped me. I reflected distractedly over a thousand different things: the dog I had as a child, a book I had read, my wife's smile, a day on the battlefield. My mind kept jumping from one vague, distant memory to another. It was like a playful kid that sniffs one bush and leaps to

Amarilla. Había en el aire un no sé qué de invitación al ensueño, al descanso, pero sobre esto, y junto con él, volaban ráfagas tenues e indescrifrables de la amenaza del hielo que no tardaría en llegar. Algo del sueño —algo de la muerte.

Mi tía andaba ocupada con sus quehaceres, y tan distraída estaba que ni me oyó entrar. Cuando le di los buenos días, dio un salto y un medio grito y me miró sobresaltada. Se compuso inmediatamente y me dijo: "No te desperté, hijo, porque creí que estarías muy cansado y que necesitabas el reposo."

No me preguntó cómo había dormido como de costumbre, por lo cual deduje que lo de anoche no se le había escapado. Pero tampoco yo quise discutir el asunto. Particularmente cuando noté que me miraba de soslayo y que mantenía una cierta distancia de mí.

Me desayuné con ganas. Ya hacía días que no tenía el apetito de esa manaña, y me alegré del desayuno de provincia que me dieron; huevos, costillas asadas, papas fritas, salsa, pan tostado y queso de vaca asado con azúcar. Comí mucho. Parecía que quería llenar comiendo un vacío interior o esconder algo feo. Parece que el cuerpo mismo se defiende de la muerte cuando el espíritu falla. Yo comía y mi tía me miraba en silencio.

Nuestra conversación quiso ser pero no fue. No teníamos qué decirnos, o más bien, no podíamos o no queríamos decírnoslo. Salí a la calle en cuanto terminé. Me encontraba desalmado, sin espíritu, sin aliento. Quise pensar de lo de anoche pero el pensamiento se me escapaba, es decir, en lo concreto. Mi mente vagaba distraída sobre mil cosas insignificantes: el perro que tuve de niño, un libro que había leído, una sonrisa de mi mujer, un día de guerra. Saltaba mi mente de recuerdo en recuerdo lejano y vago pero no se detenía en ninguno como cabrito juguetón que

another while the shepherd chases after it in vain. So I pursued my intelligence without being able to overtake it. It was as if my own intellect was afraid of me and fled from me and from the conflict I carried within. In this state of mind, or lack of it, I set out for my Uncle Rock's store.

Since my earliest recollection, this store has never changed. Let progress and evolution come and go everywhere else, the store continues to be what it has always been, a commercial institution to serve the cattlemen of Tierra Amarilla Valley. It has everything: food stuffs, clothing, yard goods, seeds, machinery, tools—everything necessary for the sheepherder or the rancher. All these things lie about in a state of well-ordered confusion. A mixture of odors, some pleasant, some not, hangs over the place. This aroma, which has penetrated the merchandise and even the walls themselves, is a combination of freshly ground coffee, hides, tobacco, and innumerable other things. Behind the store is the warehouse where great quantities of merchandise are kept, together with the cowhides and sheep pelts that have been taken in trade.

Uncle Rock's store has always been the meeting place, the social center of the town, where the men gather to pass the time. In the sun or shade of the porch in the summer. Around the huge stove inside during the winter. There they chew tobacco, spit on the firewood, and discuss the weather, the harvest, the cattle. Sometimes they relate their experiences and tell stories or riddles. There are no smutty stories or off-color jokes. My uncle would have thrown out anybody who violated his strict code of conduct; in fact, he did so on several occasions. My Uncle Rock has been dead now for many years, but my Uncle Victor demands the same

olfatea un arbusto y da un salto a otro en seguida mientras el pastor corretea en vano tras de él. Así perseguía yo a mi inteligencia sin lograr alcanzarla. Era como si mi inteligencia misma me tuviera miedo y huyera de mí, de la lucha que yo traía conmigo. En este estado de ánimo, o falta de él, me dirigí hacia la tienda de mi tío Roque.

Desde que yo me acuerdo esta tienda no ha cambiado nada. Vayan y vengan progresos y evoluciones por todas partes, ella sigue siendo lo que siempre ha sido, una institución comercial para el servicio del ganadero del valle de Tierra Amarilla. Hay en ella de todo: comestibles, ropas, paños, semillas, maquinaria, herramientas, todo lo necesario para el borreguero o ranchero. Todo esto se encuentra siempre en un estado de desarreglo arreglado. Sobre todo hay un mezcla de aromas más o menos agradable, que ya ha penetrado hasta en las mercancías y paredes mismas, de café recién molido, de vaqueta, de tabaco y un sin fin de cosas. Detrás de la tienda está la trastienda donde se guardan las cantidades grandes de mercancía, los cueros de res y las zaleas de borrega que se reciben en trato.

La tienda de don Roque ha sido siempre el punto de reunión, el centro social, donde se agregan todos los hombres a matar la vida. En la resolana o sombra del portal en el verano. Alrededor del tremendo calentón adentro en el invierno. Allí mascan tabaco, escupiendo sobre la leña, y discuten el tiempo, la cosecha, el ganado. Algunas veces cuentan sus experiencias, o cuentos, o adivinanzas. Todo esto en un plano moral y respetuoso. Mi tío habría botado al que se saliera de la estricta moral católica, y lo hizo en varias ocasiones. Ya hacía muchos años que mi tío Roque había muerto, pero mi tío Víctor demandaba el mismo respeto y

respect and maintains the same regulations. People often said it seemed as if Uncle Rock had never died.

Since it was August, I found the men on the porch, sitting on the benches and the steps or leaning against the wall. They were engaged in an animated discussion of the relative values of two saddle horses. They greeted me with affection when I came up and then renewed their argument, even asking my opinion. I sighed with relief, for I had been afraid they might know what had happened the night before. In Tierra Amarilla, news moves with a phenomenal and inexplicable speed. I smiled, thinking about the discretion of my family and its insistence on keeping its skeletons at home.

Soon bored with the rustic talk, I went into the store to get some cigarettes. My Uncle Victor was alone. He raised his eyes at the sound of the bell fastened to the door to indicate the entrance and departure of customers. His glance was half evasive, half inquisitorial. His expression invited confidence.

"Good morning, Alex. How are you this morning?"

"Very well, thanks. How are you?"

"Well . . . not too well. I couldn't get to sleep at all last night. I tossed and turned all night long."

I did not answer. I knew what was bothering him. I waited a moment and he went on,

"You produced a fine book, worthy of yourself and of your father. I am sure it will bring you money and a big reputation, but. . . ."

Once more he stopped, expecting me to say something. But I was in no mood for confidences that morning. The only thing I wanted at the moment was a cigarette. I went behind the counter and helped myself. I held out the money to my uncle, who refused

mantenía el mismo régimen. Mucha gente decía que parecía que mi tío Roque nunca había muerto.

Siendo agosto, encontré la tertulia en el portal sentados en los bancos, en los escalones, y arrimados a la pared. Tenían una discusión animada sobre los valores relativos de dos caballos de silla. Al acercarme me saludaron con cariño y reanudaron su querella, y hasta me pidieron mi parecer. Suspiré con alivio porque había temido que se hubieran enterado de lo de anoche porque en Tierra Amarilla las noticas tienen una velocidad fenomenal e inexplicable. Me sonreí al pensar en la discreción de mi familia y en su deseo de guardar sus esqueletos en casa.

Me aburrí pronto de las ramplonerías del días y entré en la tienda a comprar unos cigarros. Mi tío Victor estaba solo y alzó los ojos cuando sonó el timbre que tenía en la puerta para indicar las entradas y salidas de la gente. Su mirada fue entre esquiva e inquisidora. Su expresión invitaba confidencias.

—Buenos días, Alex. ¿Cómo amaneciste?

—Muy bien gracias, ¿y usted?

—Pues no muy bien. Se me espantó el sueño anoche y no hice más que darme vueltas casi toda la noche.

No le respondí. Ya sabía de qué pie cojeaba. Esperé un momento y continuó.

—Hiciste un buen libro, digno de tí y de tu padre. Estoy seguro que te ha de traer fama y fortuna, pero. . .

Otra vez se detuvo, esperando algo de mí. Pero yo no estaba para confidencias esa mañana. Todo lo que yo quería al momento era un cigarro y pasé detrás del mostrador y me suplí de los que quería. Le pasé el dinero a mi tío y me lo rechazó con una sonrisa

it with a smile that was too affectionate. That was a bad sign. My uncle did not ordinarily act that way. The pause was beginning to be embarrassing, but I had nothing to say, and my uncle found no words to speak. In silence, I offered him a cigarette.

"No, thanks. You know, your work moved me deeply. That's why I couldn't sleep. I can't believe that my brother Alexander was the way you say, but neither can I refuse to believe it. He is an Alexander completely different from the one I knew, the one we all knew. Nevertheless, the one you presented to us last night was no less real. Can one person be two beings, or more?"

Before I could answer and while I was trying to formulate a reasonable reply, the door of the store opened and Doña Luz came in with her little granddaughter. I thanked God. I greeted the lady and said goodbye to my uncle. I saw that he did not want me to go, but I hurried out into the street, for I was feeling a strange distress that filled me with fear. I walked swiftly to the house, got my fishing rod, and without saying anything to anyone, climbed into my car and started for Rincón. Perhaps there I would be able to calm myself or overcome my adversary, who was beginning to stir in the depths of my soul.

Probably for the first time in my life, I neither saw nor felt the beauty of that landscape which had always thrilled me so. I was no longer a part of it, as I had always been. I was now alien to the nature that surrounded me. I was on a different plane from that which lives and dies and is born again without pain, that which laughs and sings both in life and in death. I was a gloomy spirit, riven and tortured, a soul suspended between life and death, belonging to neither.

How beautifully nature clothes herself and what a smiling face she assumes when she is going to die! It is probably because she

demasiado cariñosa. Andaban mal las cosas. Mi tío no acostumbraba esos gestos. La pausa empezaba a hacerse bochornosa, pero yo no tenía nada que decir, y mi tío no hallaba cómo. En silencio le ofrecí un cigarro.

—No gracias. Sabes que tu obra me ha commovido mucho. Por eso no pude dormir. No puedo creer que mi hermano Alejandro fuera como tú dices, pero tampoco puedo no creelo. Es un Alejandro completamente distinto al que yo conocí, al que conocieron todos. No obstante el que tú nos presentaste anoche no era menos real. ¿Es que una persona puede ser dos, o más?

Antes que yo pudiera contestar, y mientras trataba de formular una contestación racional, se abrió la puerta de la tienda y entró doña Luz y su nietecita. Di gracias a Dios. Saludé a la señora y me despedí de mi tío. Vi que se quedó muy insatisfecho. Salí a la calle precipitadamente porque ya sentía unas congojas extrañas que me llenaban de temor. Caminé rápidamente a la casa, cogí mi vara de pescar, y sin hablarle a nadie me subí en el coche y me dirigí al Rincón. Quizá allí podría tranquilizarme o vencer a mi adversario que ya empezaba a moverse en las profundidades de mi alma.

Quizá por la primera vez en mi vida no vi ni sentí aquel paisaje que siempre me había llenado de alegría. No, ni fui parte de él como siempre lo había sido. Ahora yo era cosa extraña a la naturaleza que me rodeaba. Me encontraba en un plano distinto a lo que vive y muere y vuelve a nacer sin dolor, a lo que ríe y canta mientras vive y muere. Yo era una alma triste, partida y torturada, una alma suspendida entre la vida y la muerte que ni vivía ni moría.

¡Qué linda se viste y qué risueña se pone la naturaleza cuando va a morir! Será porque sabe que volverá a nacer, que las glorias

knows that the glories of today will be repeated next year and the year after eternally. It may be because she knows that after the winter comes spring, that death is neither sorrow nor the end, but a rest and a beginning. She can live because she has not the slightest fear of death. I feared it; therefore I could not live. My father had courted death and received its caresses. And today my father, though dead, was living! I, alive, was dying!

I found myself opening a fence gate on that violated land which had remained virgin as long as it belonged to our family. Then he spoke to me.

"Oh, Allie, if you only knew how every one of those fence posts hurt me as long as I lived! Each one was a stake driven into my very heart."

His arrival did not surprise me, for I had been expecting it. I replied with irritation.

"Don't call me Allie. I am not a child." But, looking at that barbed wire, I felt as he had, and I added,

"You are right about the fence. It is a crime against nature and against God. It is stupid for a man to believe that a piece of land belongs to him. He prides himself on it, takes out papers to prove his ownership, puts up fences, and constructs buildings without realizing that all this is in vain. The land was there long before he was, and it will be there when he is dead. It will continue to be when there is no longer the slightest evidence that he ever existed. Rather, the land owns the man, for it consumes him, digests him, annihilates him." I had read all this somewhere.

"So we are in a mood for speeches! Right out in the middle of the road in the bright sunlight. Come on. Get in, and let's go. You let someone see you talking to yourself, and he will think you are crazy. And he wouldn't be too far off."

de hoy se repetirán mañana, y pasado mañana, eternamente. Será porque sabe que después del invierno viene la primavera, que la muerte no es el dolor ni el fin sino el descanso y el comienzo. No le tiene ningún temor a la muerte por eso puede vivir. Yo temía a la muerte y por eso no podía vivir. Mi padre cortejó a la muerte y recibió sus caricias. ¡Y hoy mi padre vivía muerto! !Yo moría vivo!

Me encontré abriendo la puerta de una cerca en aquella tierra ultrajada que había sido virgen mientras fue nuestra. Entonces me habló.

—Ay, Alejandrito, si supieras el dolor que me causó cada uno de esos postes. Cada uno fue una estaca clavada en mi propio corazón.

No me sorprendió su llegada, que bien anticipada la tenía. Le respondí con cierta irritación.

—No me digas Alejandrito. No soy niño—. Mas al ver aquellas púas del alambrado sentí lo que mi padre había sentido, y añadí: En esto tienes razón. Es un crimen contra la naturaleza y contra Dios. Es una estupidez que un hombre crea que un pedazo de tierra le pertenezca. Se jacta en ello, saca papeles para probarlo, le pone cercas, y levanta fincas sin darse cuenta que todo esto es por demás. Antes que él la tierra fue, y cuando él deje de ser, ella todavía será, y continuará siendo cuando ya no haya vestigio alguno de que él existió. Más bien posee la tierra al hombre porque ella se lo come, lo digiere, lo aniquila. —Esto lo había leído yo en alguna parte.

—Para oradores estamos. En medio del camino y en pleno sol. Súbete en ese buque y vamos, no te vaya a ver alguien hablando solo y crea que estás loco. No andaría del todo desorientado.

The absurdity of the situation struck me like a kiss from a flabby old woman, and I had to laugh. Laughter bubbled up from him—irresistible, contagious laughter—and I laughed with him. Meanwhile, far back on the borders of consciousness, a little voice was asking, "Can it be that I am really crazy?" I smothered it under another guffaw. Finally the outbursts began to diminish, but before I could reflect on the illogical thing that was happening, my father said,

"Let's go over to the big rocks on your Uncle Ishmael's ranch. There are some good fishing holes there."

"No. We are going to our old ranch." I felt the need to impose my will.

"You know very well that there is no quiet water. Besides, you can't fish there."

"Why not?"

"You'll see."

At that moment, we reached the place where the road turns off toward our old ranch house. The first thing I saw was a big sign that read, "No trespassing." His ironic laughter made me decide to enter in spite of the sign, but when I tried to open the big gate, I met a padlock that admitted no arguments.

I started off raging, and the dust cloud I raised was a witness to my state of mind. I was still determined not to go where my father told me, and I passed the place—in silence, for he said nothing. When I reached the bend in the river, I almost drove into it. There was no bridge! A flood had carried it away. I was so angry that a "Damn you!" escaped my lips.

Whether I wanted to or not, I ended up at the fishing holes on my Uncle Ishmael's ranch, where I had intended to go in the first place. I was still furious, and for a long time I busied myself

Lo ridículo de la situación me dio en la cara como beso de vieja atrevida y tuve que reírme. Monté en el coche y seguí mi camino, es decir, seguimos nuestro camino. Le retosaba la risa, aquella risa contagiosa que no se podía resistir, y yo le accompañaba. Entretanto, allá en los detrases de mi conciencia una vocecita me preguntaba: "¿Estaré loco de veras?" Yo la ahogaba con una nueva carcajada. Por fin empezaron a disminuir las explosiones, pero antes que yo pudiera reflexionar sobre lo irracional de lo que acontecía, dijo mi padre:

—Vamos allá a las piedras grandes en el rancho de tu tío Ismael. Hay unos pozos muy buenos allí.

—No, vamos al rancho de nosotros—. Sentí la necesidad de imponer mi voluntad.

—Ya tú sabes que allí no hay buenos remansos, y además, no se puede pescar allí.

—Por qué no?

—Ya verás.

En esto llegamos adonde se aparta el camino para la antigua casa de campo nuestra. Lo primero que vi fue tamaño rótulo que decía: "No se permite entrar." Su risita irónica me decidió entrar a pesar del letrero, pero cuando quise abrir el puertón me encontré con un candado que no admitía argumentos. Salí de ahí muy fastidiado, y la polvareda que levanté fue testimonio de ello. Iba determinado a no ir a donde mi padre me decía, y me pasé del lugar —en silencio, porque él no chistaba. Cuando llegué a la vuelta del río, por poco caigo en él. ¡No tenía puente! se lo había llevado una venida. Mi rabia fue tal que se me escapó un "¡Mal rayo te parta!"

Quiera que no quiera fui a dar a los pozos del rancho de mi tío Ismael, adonde había intentado ir en primer lugar. Andaba

baiting my hooks in silence. Little by little, my anger died down. I began to remember the jolly picnics my family used to have in this very place in a romantic, and even more romanticized, past. A feeling of nostalgia for those bygone days, for those beloved beings now deceased, for the many dreams I had left buried here filled my heart and overflowed my eyes.

"You are very funny. How easily you jump from philosophical lawyer to sentimental poet!"

"Don't you feel a little of what I feel?"

"Not at all, Alex. Not only do I not feel as you do anymore; I do not feel at all."

"Then I am convinced that you are an imposter or, to be more exact, a fraud. Anyone who feels no emotion on this land is not a Turriaga, much less my father."

"You are mistaken. You forget that those sentiments and the tie you feel with the people and with the land are things of the flesh, of the heart. Having neither body nor heart, I find myself above those outworn devotions and free of them. I understand them, but I do not feel them. And I find them a little ridiculous, unworthy of the spirit."

This statement made me quite thoughtful. It was a new facet of this spiritual being that threatened me, something I would have to take into account if I expected to overcome him. If he was incapable of human feelings, I would attack him in the realm of the intellect.

"Cast your hook near that big rock yonder, just where that ray of sunlight strikes. There is a big one over there."

"I don't want to." I was insisting on going my independent way. It was necessary not to let myself be controlled in the

rabiando y por largo rato me ocupé en ensartar mis anzuelos en silencio. Poco a poco se me fue bajando la calentura y empecé a recordar los alegres días de campo que mi familia había tenido en este mismo sitio en un pasado romántico y más romantizado. Un sentimiento de nostalgia por aquellos días muertos, por aquellos seres queridos, y difuntos, por los muchos sueños que aquí dejé sepultados, me llenó el alma y quiso rebosarme por los ojos.

—Gracioso estás. Con qué facilidad saltas de abogado filósofo a poeta sentimental.

—¿A poco tú no sientes lo que yo?

—Lejos de ello, Alejandrito. No sólo no siento como tú sino que no siento del todo.

—Entonces quedo convencido de que eres un impostor, o mejor, una mentira. El que no se siente emocionado en esta sierra no es Turriaga, y mucho menos mi padre.

—Te equivocas y olvidas que esos sentimientos y apego que tú sientes hacia las personas y hacia la tierra son cosas de la carne, del estómago. No teniendo ni carne ni estómago, yo me encuentro en un plano superior a esas querencias caducas y libre de ellas. Las comprendo pero no las siento, y las hallo no poco ridículas, indignas del espíritu.

Esto me puso bastante pensativo. Era una faceta nueva de este ser espiritual que me amenazaba, algo que tendría que tomar en cuenta si esperaba vencerle. Si era incapaz de sentimientos humanos, le atacaría en el reino intelectual.

—Pon el anzuelo junto a la piedra aquella, ahí donde pega ese rayito de luz. Ahí está una grande.

—No quiero—. Me empeñaba en seguir mi vía independiente.

slightest. My free will, already threatened, was resisting this latest usurpation.

With this resolution, I kept on fishing and thinking, throwing my line everywhere except the place he had pointed out. And I did not catch a thing. I didn't even have a nibble. Meanwhile, that accursed stone and that confounded ray of light attracted me in spite of my determination. Over and over I found myself looking at them out of the corner of my eye. I would look away, only to cast sidelong glances in that direction again. When this happened, I scolded myself furiously. But I had to admit that something stronger than I was leading me where I did not want to go.

All this time, my father kept quiet, but the strength of his will was weighing heavily upon me. Conscious of that fact, I redoubled my determination not to yield.

Suddenly, I tossed the hook where I had not wanted to put it. Immediately I caught a big one. Forgetting my defeat for a moment, I uttered a yelp of joy and devoted myself to pulling in my catch. When I had succeeded, I stood gazing at it proudly.

"Didn't I tell you?" My father's voice was ironically triumphant.

His words hit me like a whiplash. Instantly I remembered that I had let myself be worsted. How bitter is the taste of humiliation! In the excitement of gaining a bagatelle, I had lost a soul, I had bartered my integrity, I had allowed myself to be manipulated by alien forces—and for a moment, I had enjoyed my own defeat!

A raging fury seized me, the fury that devours because it begins and ends in the one who engenders it. It has no escape, it is not spent, it putrifies for lack of ventilation.

I seized the cursed fish and hurled it into the water, at the foot of the rock with the ray of sunlight, now a symbol of something

Era necesario que yo no me dejara vencer ni en lo más mínimo. Mi albedrío, ya amendazado, se resistía a esta nueva usurpación.

Con este tesón seguí pescando y pensando, poniendo el anzuelo en todas partes menos en el lugar que se me había señalado. Y no pesqué nada. Ni picó una siquiera. Entre tanto aquella maldita piedra, y aquel condenado rayito de luz, me atraían a pesar de mi resolución. De continuo me hallaba mirándolos del rabo del ojo, y entonces miraba para otro lado, para volver a ojearlos de soslayo. Cuando esto ocurría, me reñía con furia. Más porque tenía que admitir que algo más fuerte que yo me llevaba a donde no quería ir.

En todo esto mi padre guardaba silencio, pero la fuerza de su voluntad pesaba ya sobre mí. Consciente de ello, me determinaba yo una vez más a no ceder.

De repente puse el anzuelo donde no había querido ponerlo, e immediatamente se cogió un animalón. Di un grito de alegría, olvidando por el momento mi derrota, y me dediqué a sacarlo. Cuando lo hice, lo contemplé con orgullo.

—¿No te lo dije? —me dijo mi padre con ironía y triunfo.

Sus palabras me dieron en la cara como un azote. Me recordaron de pronto que me había dejado vencer. Cuán amargo es el sabor de la ignominia. En el estímulo de la conquista de una bagatela había yo perdido una alma, había vendido mi integridad, me había dejado dominar por fuerzas extrañas a mí —y por un momento hasta había gozado de mi derrota.

Me arrebató una rabia mala. La rabia que devora porque empieza y acaba en el que la engendra, que no tiene salida, que no se agota, que se pudre por falta de ventilación.

Cogí el maldito pescado y lo arrojé al agua, a la piedra con el

horrible. I began to curse and to weep. To weep with dry, scorching, silent tears. Tears that are never seen, but that surge upward and burn within the heart.

In the heavy air about me, my father was laughing. And the white belly of the fish, undulating on the water, accused me. My rage and my shame gnawed at each other—or kissed one another.

In the depths of my consciousness, the figure of my wife began to emerge as a liberating image. Thinking about her, leaning on her memory, I found strength enough to return to my uncle's house and the supper which I badly needed.

CHAPTER IV

After a night filled with bad dreams and worse wakefulness, I decided to go home. I said goodbye to my uncle and aunt during breakfast. In spite of their many expressions of affection, I could not help observing a relief so great they could not hide it. I had to admit that I was making their lives quite complicated. Nevertheless, the relief was not all on their side. I, too, felt myself stimulated and hopeful, now that I was leaving. I wanted to get away at once from that house, that atmosphere, which had treated me in such a tragic way.

I set out with a feeling of exuberance. All my hopes of peace and tranquility were now fixed on my wife and my home. I had proved to myself definitively the day before that I could not depend on my own strength. I thought that once outside that atmosphere so steeped in the personality of my father, once again

rayito de luz, símbolo ahora de algo feo. Me puse a llorar y a maldecir. A llorar con lágrimas secas, calcinantes y silenciosas. Lágrimas que no se ven pero que surcan y queman.

Y en el éter pesado que me rodeaba mi padre se reía. Y la panza blanca del pescado ondulaba en el agua, y también me acusaba. Mi rabia y mi vergüenza se mordían o se besaban.

Allá en el fondo de mi inteligencia empezó a surgir la figura de mi mujer como una imagen salvadora. Pensando en ella, apoyándome en su memoria, hallé las fuerzas para volver a casa de mis tíos, y a la cena que malamente necesitaba.

CAPITULO IV

Después de una noche llena de malos sueños y de peor insomnio, decidí marcharme a mi casa. Me despedí de mis tíos durante el desayuno. A pesar de sus muchas muestras de cariño no pude menos que observar el grande alivio que no pudieron ocultar. Tuve que admitir que yo les estaba complicando la vida demasiado. No obstante, el alivio no fue todo de ellos. Yo también me sentía un tanto estimulado y esperanzado con mi partida. Quería salir cuanto antes de aquella casa, de aquel ambiente, que tan trágicamente me había usado.

Me puse en camino con cierta exuberancia. Todas mis esperanzas de sosiego y tranquilidad estaban ahora puestas en mi mujer y en mi casa. Ya se me había demostrado definitivamente ayer que no podía contar con mis propias fuerzas. Creía que una vez fuera de este ambiente tan empapado con la personalidad de

in surroundings which I dominated, once more absorbed in the reality which was my Mima, I would recover my equilibrium and my normality.

I remembered again with a joy bordering on madness the many times I had found refuge and comfort in Mima's arms—times when, crushed and sorrowful, I had seen the storms of life destroy my most sacred illusions and ambitions. On the tempestuous sea of my personal reality, she, only she, stood always firm and invincible. How many times in moments of passion I had said to her, "You are my only reality!" And it was true. As a young man and even when I was older, I used to go about with my head in the clouds, losing all contact with things as they are and will always be. At those times, she set me gently back on the solid base of truth—always preventing me from suffering the shock of a fall.

Now that my mind was wandering through worlds of fantasy or illusion, I needed my wife more than ever. She would not fail me. She never had failed me. My confidence increased as I drew nearer to her.

While I was musing thus, sustaining my entire being on what I hoped and dreamed might be, back in the dim recesses of my consciousness hovered the disquiet which I now recognized as the presence of my father. I kept trying to forget that presence, telling myself that it was not there. It was like trying to ignore a persistent nausea that does not permit itself to be forgotten.

Surely the love that existed between Mima and me, the home that we had built together, the mutual personality that we shared—all positive realities—would be enough to conquer this specter born of nothing. The nothingness of memory and imagination, whose own reality was doubtful. My father, who was dead, had waylaid me, the living, in cowardly fashion. His lust for

mi padre, que una vez puesto en un ambiente que yo dominara, que tan pronto como absorbiera la realidad que era mi Mima, recobraría mi equilibrio y mi normalidad.

Recordé una vez más con una alegría que frisaba en la locura las muchas veces que había hallado refugio y consuelo en los brazos de Mima cuando abatido y triste veía las tormentas de la vida destrozar mis más sagradas ilusiones y ambiciones. En ese mar tempestuoso de mi realidad, ella, sólo ella, permanecía firme e invencible. ¡Cuántas veces le había dicho en nuestros momentos apasionados: "Tú eres mi única realidad!" Y en verdad. De joven, y después, de viejo, cuando solía yo algunas veces andar con la cabeza en las nubes, cuando perdía contacto con lo que es, con lo que siempre será, ella me ponía suavemente en la solidez de la verdad —evitándome siempre el golpe de la caída.

Ahora que mi cabeza, y todo lo que había, o no había en ella, vagaba por esos mundos de la ilusión o fantasía, o lo que fuera, sin orientación ninguna, ahora era cuando necesitaba yo a mi mujer más que nunca. Y no me faltaría. Jamás me había faltado. Mi confianza crecía conforme me acercaba a ella.

Mientras así divagaba, apoyando todo mi ser en lo que yo esperaba y quería que fuera, allá en los detrases de mi conciencia se revolteaba la congoja que ya conocía como la presencia de mi padre. Trataba de olvidar su presencia, haciéndome creer que no estaba allí, como el que trata de ignorar un mareo persistente que no se deja ignorar.

Seguramente el amor que existía entre Mima y yo, el hogar que nos habíamos hecho, la mutua personalidad que compartíamos, realidades positivas todas, podrían vencer este espectro hecho de la nada. La nada de la memoria y de la imaginación, cuya realidad era dudosa. Mi padre, muerto, me acechó a mí, vivo,

life was trying to rob me of my existence. He took advantage of the affection I had for him to destroy me. He was the past, the dead. The essence of his being was negative and immoral, and that fact would lead to his destruction.

But what about the big fishing holes? What about the trout? Those wretched questions surged up to torment me and prove to me that my will had already been subjugated. And the face in the wine glass. . . . You saw it. It was yours, but it was not you. . . . And your voice, your laughter, your wit. You can no longer convince yourself that they were yours, that what happened was only the result of your aberrant imagination. You have to accept it; it was your father. There is no doubt. Your father is stronger than you. Then what or who are you now, if you are not you? Are you or are you not your father? With whom are you talking right now? With yourself? Then are you two other people besides your father? And who is observing and worrying about all this? A third or fourth you who watches this tragic jest from a reserved seat? And what are the names of all those *yous*? Alex, Alexander Senior, Alexis, Alexander Junior, Allie!

"Mima! Mima!"

"For heaven's sake, Allie, calm down! It isn't so bad. I know you have a serious problem, but with a little good sense and intelligence, you—I mean we—will be O.K."

I took a long time about answering, not only because I did not know what to say, but also because I was on the verge of losing control of the car. It was off the road, traveling at high speed. When I had the vehicle under control and had calmed my jangled nerves a little, I addressed my father—or, rather, myself.

"So now you know. Just wait until we get home, and you will see what becomes of you!"

cobardemente, y su codicia de vida quería robarme la mía. Se aprovechó del cariño que yo le tenía para así quitarme la vida. El era el pasado, lo muerto. Lo negativo e inmoral eran la esencia de su ser, y ello le destruiría.

¿Pero lo de los pozos grandes? ¿Lo de la trucha? Estas desgraciadas preguntas venían a atormentarme y demostrarme a cada momento que ya mi voluntad había sido subyugada. Y la cara en la copa de vino. Tú la viste. Era la tuya, pero no eras tú . . . Y su voz, su risa, su burla. No podías ya convencerte que eran tuyas, que era tu imaginación extraviada. Tenías que aceptarlo: tu padre era. No cabía duda. Tu padre era más que tú ¿Entonces, qué o quién eres tú si no eres tú? ¿Eres o no eres tu padre? ¿Con quién hablas ahora? ¿Contigo? ¿Entonces eres dos además de ser tu padre? ¿Y quién observa y se preocupa de todo esto? ¿Un tercer o cuarto tú que contempla esta tragi-burla de un asiento de preferencia? ¿Cómo se llaman todos estos tús? ¡Alex! ¡Alejandro! ¡Alejandrito! ¡Alejandrillo! ¡Alejandrico!

—¡Mima! ¡Mima!—

—Por Dios, Alejandrito, cálmate. No es para tanto. Ya sé que tu problema es grande, pero con un poco de buen sentido y otra tanta inteligencia quedarás, es decir, quedaremos bien.

Me tardé en contestar, no sólo porque no hallaba qué decir, sino también porque ya estaba para perder por completo el dominio del coche. Este ya iba a una velocidad espantosa y fuera del camino. Cuando hube dominado el vehículo y calmado un poco mis nervios alarmados, me dirigí a mi padre, o mejor dicho, a mí.

—Conque ya sabes. Aguarda a que lleguemos a casa y verás lo que será de tí.

"If you aren't careful, you won't get home. Keep on driving in the ditch at ninety miles an hour, and you will soon reach a place where you will be with me forever. Take my word for it. No matter how bad this situation may seem, it is a thousand times better than the darkness, the silence, and the motionless stagnation of the place I come from. Here, at least, there is light, there is life, there is struggle."

"What good is light to me if I have to see it from a prison? What good is life if it is someone else's? Or struggle if I must lose?"

"If you persist with those wild ideas, you will drive yourself crazy. As a mad man, you are no good either to yourself or to me. So watch those ugly moods and fits of temper."

"Even madness would be welcome if it would free me of you. I will seek freedom in an asylum if there is no other way. If I can't get rid of you even there, perhaps in mental emptiness I may learn to endure, possibly even love you."

"Don't say such crazy things!"

The irritation in his voice showed me that the situation had changed. Now he was the one on the defensive. The idea of my death or lunacy filled him with terror. If I died, he died. If my mind failed, he died also, since he lived only in my intelligence.

This fact filled me with a macabre complacency. For a morbid moment, I considered suicide and a life of insanity. I would be free of his insufferable presence; I would get rid of this intellectual delirium; I would find peace at last.

But what about Mima, oh, man of little faith? Ah, my wife. . . . Remember the war, those days which were as black as this one. In the midst of danger, she filled you with courage and confidence. Have you perchance lost the inner resources you counted on at

—Si no te cuidas, ni llegarás a casa siquiera. Sigue conduciendo por los arroyos a noventa millas por hora y pronto llegarás a donde nunca te despedirás de mí. Toma mi consejo. Por malo que te parezca esto, es mil veces mejor que la obscuridad, el estancamiento, el silencio y la inmovilidad de donde yo vengo. Aquí por lo menos hay luz, hay vida, hay lucha.

—¿De qué me sirve la luz si la he de ver desde una prisión? ¿La vida si ha de ser ajena? ¿La lucha si la he de perder?

—Si te empeñas en esas tonterías enloquecerás de seguro. Loco, ni te sirves a tí ni a mí. De modo que cuidado con esos humores y genios.

—Hasta la locura apetecería si así me libraba de tí. Si no logro desasirme de tí de otra manera, lo buscaré en el manicomio. Si allí no lo logro, quizá aprenda a soportarte, posiblemente hasta quererte, en el vacío mental.

—¡No hables locuras! —La petulancia de su voz me indicó que la situación había cambiado. Ahora era él quien estaba en la defensiva. Mi muerte o mi locura le llenaba de terror. Si yo moría moría él. Si yo enloquecía también fallecía él, ya que sólo vivía en mi inteligencia.

Esto me dió una complacencia macabra. Contemplé por un mórbido momento el suicidio y la vida al margen de la cordura. Así me libraría de su infanda presencia, desecharía este vértigo intelectual, hallaría la paz con que se duerme y se come bien.

Pero, hombre de poca fe, ¿y Mima? Ah, mi mujer. Acuérdate de la guerra, de aquellos días tan negros como éste. En medio del peligro, ella te llenaba de valor y de confianza. ¿Acaso has perdido los recursos interiores con que contabas entonces? No. Mima

that time? No. Mima is still the fountain at which I nourish my spirit. She will give me food and drink. Then, restored, I will take my vengeance—and I will laugh with her. Together, we will shout with laughter.

My spirits were rising again. I imagined that I had only to see her and all this horror would disappear. That the evil spirit would flee the presence of the good spirit. When I thought of this, I laughed with infantile joy. I laughed like a child. And, like a child, I forgot everything else.

I was now in such a good humor that I even began to notice the road. I was crossing one of those sterile, colorless plains so frequent in New Mexico. If I had not been in such a state of mental torpor, like a sleepy child, perhaps I might have noticed that the qualities of neutrality, of sterility, reflected my own. But I did not see that fact. No. I peopled the desert with cattle and cowboys, and one of them was I. In fantasy, I saw a wild bull attacking me, but I was escaping. I was escaping from the bull and everything that threatened—and everything was escaping from me.

While I wandered in this illusory world, my car was speeding along the roads. Each moment brought me closer to my home, to my wife, to a rendezvous with my destiny. The urgency of this confrontation began to make itself felt. Little by little, I returned to the realization of my peculiar situation. Slowly I recovered my senses and my feelings. Again I faced the problem of life and death.

In the moments of greatest danger, a man gathers all his faculties about him. Mind and body achieve a superhuman harmony. Every nerve is strained, ready to spring to his defense. The whole being is caught up in that hunger for combat which

todavía es la fuente en que me nutro. Ella me dará de beber y de comer, y restablecido, me vengaré —y me reiré, con ella, juntos, a carcajadas nos reiremos.

Otra vez mi espíritu estaba en el ascenso. Me figuraba que sólo tenía que verla y todo este horror se desvanecería. Que el espíritu malo huiría de la presencia del espíritu bueno. Al pensar esto, me reí con alegría infantil. Me reí como un niño. Y, como a un niño, se me olvidó todo.

Me sentía ya de tan buen humor que hasta me empecé a fijar en el camino. Iba cruzando una de esas llanuras neutras y estériles tan frecuentes en Nuevo México. Si no me hubiera encontrado en un estado de ánimo de modorra mental, de niño con sueño, quizá habría notado que esa neutralidad, esa esterilidad, reflejaba la mía. Mas yo no notaba eso. No. Yo poblaba el desierto de reses y vaqueros, y entre ellos andaba yo. En la fantasía veía un toro bravío que me embestía, y que yo me escapaba. Me escapaba del toro y de todo. Todo se me escapaba.

Mientras yo andaba en este mundo iluso mi coche iba a toda velocidad por esos caminos. Con cada momento me acercaba más a mi casa, a mi mujer —a mi rendez-vous con mi destino. La urgencia de la cita empezó a hacerse sentir. Poco a poco empecé a darme cuenta de mi peculiar realidad. Lentamente recobré mis sentidos y sensaciones. Me enfrenté otra vez con mi problema de vida y de muerte.

En los momentos de mayor peligro el hombre reúne alrededor de sí todas sus facultades. Cobra su cuerpo y su inteligencia una armonía más que humana. Cada nervio anda de puntillas listo para saltar a la defensa. Le viene aquella ansia de combate del

the soldier feels when he has resolved to do or die and awaits the enemy.

In the midst of a new courage sparked by this overdue resolution, there arose a hunger for my wife, a clamorous, physical hunger. I wanted the fragrance, the warmth, the murmurs, the flavor of life that were in her. I wanted all this for its own sake to establish through it the fact that I was a man, if not the fact of my existence.

I could not forget there in the dark recesses of my mind that if I should die now, my existence would be forever ended. Since I had no child, even my name would disappear. I would live in the memory of a few people for a while, but then—absolute oblivion. A child! I needed a child which would carry in itself some traces of my personality, something of my being. If only my name. My thirst for life clamored to be satisfied. Almost, almost I could understand, even justify, my father's obsession.

Only Mima could give me that life in her vital kisses, or in a child. My desperation increased. The car was no longer running; it was flying. My meeting with my wife or with fate, or with both, was coming close.

What would she say when she saw me? What would I say? I was already in Albuquerque. My torment was almost over. But what about him? Where was he? It did not matter. Mima would get rid of him. How hot it was! And I was hungry. No, not hungry—thirsty. You have to watch the traffic, the people. Mima and I would sleep in peace. We would laugh. Wait! The light is red. Not a trace would remain. . . . Oh, God, do not forsake me! How long it had been since I had prayed! Since the war. Berlin. June twenty-first. In June, I began my book. Damn. . . . The light has changed. Let's go.

soldado que ya ha tomado su determinación interior y espera el enemigo.

En medio del nuevo coraje a la tardía determinación se incorporó el hambre por mi mujer, una hambre demandadora, física. Quería el olor, el calor, el rumor, y el sabor de vida que en ella había. Lo quería por sí mismo, y quizá, para establecer por ello mi razón de ser hombre, ya que no razón de ser.

Tampoco podía olvidar allá en los escondrijos de mi conciencia que si yo moría ahora, acabaría para siempre. No teniendo hijo, hasta mi nombre desaparecería. Viviría en la memoria de algunos por poco y, después, olvido absoluto. ¡Un hijo! Necesitaba un hijo que llevara en sí algunas huellas de mi personalidad, algo de mi ser. Mi nombre siquiera. Mi sed de vida clamaba por satisfacción. Casi, casi, podía comprender y justificar la obsesión de mi padre.

Sólo Mima me podía dar esa vida en sus besos vitales, o en un hijo. Mi desesperación aumentaba, y el coche no andaba, volaba. Mi entrevista con mi mujer, o con la suerte, o con ambas, estaba llegando.

¿Qué diría ella al verme? ¿Qué diría yo? Ya estaba en Albuquerque. Ya estaba para terminarse mi suplicio. ¿Y él? ¿Dónde estaba? No importaba. Mima lo despediría. Qué calor hacía aquí. Y tenía hambre. No, no hambre, sed. Hay que fijarse en el tráfico, en la gente. Mima y yo dormiríamos muy a gusto. Nos reiríamos. Espera. Está roja. No quedaría ni un vestigio . . . Dios, no me abandones. Cómo hacía que no rezaba. Desde la guerra. Berlín. 21 de junio. En junio empecé mi libro. ¡Mal rayo! . . . ya cambió. Vamos.

Fourth Street. It is only a few blocks more. I feel myself ablaze with anxiety, with fear, with hope. Almost unconscious of the people calmly crossing the streets, I darted from one block to another, impelled by a terrifying, and at the same time terrified, will to live. Desperately, I projected my being toward my wife, where I expected to find the life that was escaping me. I longed for the revivifying contact of her flesh.

There is my corner. There is my house. Mima is inside. There is a great knot in my throat. Berlin. How hot and dry my mouth is! You are the only real thing in all this world. If I ever get out of this one. . . . My knees and my lower lip tremble. Here I am.

I wanted to hurl myself at the door. I controlled myself. I would frighten Mima. I tried to hide my feelings, to recover some little equilibrium. Something was filling me with an ugly, groveling terror. I opened the door with feigned self-possession.

She was not in the living room. Everything that belonged to me leaped to greet me. Even the stain on the rug. This was mine. I was king here. Those chairs, those books. All of them, all, were a part of me. Here dwelt my memories, my successes, my failures. My gaze took in all these beloved objects. My confidence and my strength were growing fast, until. . . .

I saw the portrait of my father. My hopes fell in ruins around me. The face in the portrait and mine in the mirror behind it were the same. For a long, long time I stood fixed to the spot, stupefied. My father's ghost, now sure of me, left me alone.

Staggering, my strength drained, I went into the kitchen searching for my wife, afraid to find her. It was now late. Very late. She was not there. I went on into the bedroom. There I found her stretched out on the bed, asleep. There I found her, and there I lost her forever.

La calle cuarta. Sólo quedan unas cuantas cuadras. Me siento arder de ansiedad, de miedo, de esperanza. Casi ignorante de la gente tranquila que cruzaba las calles, yo me lanzaba de calle a calle impulsado por una aterrizadora, y a la vez aterrizada voluntad de vivir. Desesperadamente proyectaba mi ser hacia mi esposa donde esperaba hallar la vida que ya se me escapaba. Anhelaba el contacto vivificante de su carne.

Allí está mi esquina. Allí esta mi casa. Adentro está Mima. Y en la garganta tengo un nudo. Berlín. Qué seca y qué caliente traigo la boca. Tú eres lo único real en el mundo. Si salgo de ésta . . . Me tiemblan las rodillas y el labio inferior. Aquí estoy.

Quise arrojarme a la puerta. Me contuve. Asustaría a Mima. Traté de disimular, de recobrar algún equilibrio cualquiera. Algo me llenaba de un terror servil y feo. Abrí la puerta con aplomo falso.

No estaba en la sala. Todo lo mío saltó a saludarme. Hasta la mancha en la alfombra. Esto era mío. Aquí mandaba yo. Esas sillas, esos libros. Todo, todo, era parte de mí. Aquí moraban mis recuerdos, mis éxitos, mis fracasos. Mi vista recorría todos estos objetos amados y mi confianza y mis fuerzas se doblaban, hasta que . . .

Vi el retrato de mi padre. Me corté. La cara del retrato y la mía en el espejo detrás de él eran la misma. Por largo, largo rato quedé clavado, lelo. El espectro de mi padre, seguro de sí, me dejaba solo.

Trastrabillando, aniquilado, entré en la cocina buscando a mi esposa y temiendo hallarla. Ya era tarde. Muy tarde. No estaba ahí. Pasé a la recámara. Ahí la encontré, tumbada sobre la cama, dormida. Allí la hallé, y la perdí para siempre.

I stared at her in silence for a long time. Because I did not have the strength to wake her. Because I had no desire to do so. It did not matter any longer. Like death, she had a fatal fascination for me. The woman on the bed, my wife Mima, was not my wife. It was not Mima. It was my dead mother!

How long I stood there dully, my mind a blank, I do not know. Suddenly I found myself on the floor and I heard, as from a great distance, the horror-stricken cry of a doomed man. Something—I do not know what—told me that this cry was my own. Then shadows, from whose depths came a tortured scream from Mima—from my mother. The cry, vague and confused, grew weaker and weaker in the blackness and space that undulated about me. Only the echo remained, and I moved with the echo. Together we were lost in the blankness of nothing.

Long, long afterwards, moments or centuries afterwards, I appeared before a macabre court. My father, dressed in black, was the judge. Each member of the jury carried in his hand a black whip which he kept continually cracking. Each snap produced a sound so revolting that it began to fascinate me. I moved closer, only to recoil in horror and repugnance. Those whips were long, black human tongues! But I had no time to dwell on that, because suddenly bells started tolling. The jury began to chant in unison with the monotonous strokes, beating time with their terrifying whips. "A-lex—is—cra-zy. A-lex—is—cra-zy."

All these things confused and baffled me. I sought help and sympathy in the faces that surrounded me. But when I thought I recognized the face of someone, the features disintegrated in an attempt to smile. All that remained was a formless, moving mass that defied recognition.

I stood passive and irresolute while the first witness testified in

La contemplé en silencio por mucho tiempo. Porque no tenía las fuerzas para despertarla. Porque carecía de voluntad. Ya no importaba. Me fascinaba fatalmente esta mujer, como la muerte. La mujer sobre la cama, mi esposa, Mima, no era mi esposa, no era Mima. ¡Era mi difunta madre!

Cuanto tiempo permanecí allí, negativo y borrado, no sé. De repente me encontré en el suelo y oí venir como de muy lejos el grito horrendo de un condenado. Algo, no sé qué, me dijo que ese grito era mío. Luego tinieblas, de cuyas profundidades salía el atormentado grito de Mima, de mi madre, "¡Hijo mío, hijo mío!" Confuso e indefinido el grito de ella se perdía cada vez más en la negrura y en la lejanía que ondulaban en mi redor. Sólo quedó el eco y con el eco me fuí yo, y juntos nos perdimos en la nada de la nada.

Mucho, mucho después, momentos o siglos después me presenté ante un lúgubre tribunal. Mi padre era el juez, vestido de negro. Los miembros del jurado tenían cada uno un negro látigo en la mano que chasqueaban de continuo. Cada latigazo producía un chasquido muy desagradable, tanto que empezó a fascinarme de una manera irresistible. Fui acercándome sólo para recular lleno de horror y repugnancia. ¡Esos látigos eran largas y negras lenguas humanas! Pero no tuve tiempo de permanecer en esto porque de pronto empezaron a doblar campanas. El jurado empezó a cantar en coro al son de los toques monótonos, al compás de sus azotes aterradores, "El Alex está loco. El Alex está loco."

Todo esto me confundía y me frustraba. Buscaba apoyo y simpatía en las caras que me rodeaban. Pero cuando creía que conocía la cara de alguien, ésta se deshacía al sonreír, y sólo quedaba una masa informe y movible que se desesperaba queriendo ser.

my defense. Her testimony was even more devastating. She was saying that I was not crazy, but that I had two heads! This statement stunned me, especially when the jury began to chant as they cracked their whips to the rhythm. "He-has-two-heads." Then, "Cut-off-one. Cut-off-one!"

I tried to speak in my own behalf, but nobody paid any attention to me. Nobody understood me, and I did not understand myself. The judge came running with a mirror and gave it to me. It was true! I did have two heads. One of them was mine; the other was my father's. I fainted away.

Floating on clouds of black smoke, I rose and fell and knew nothing. But I kept hearing the crack of long tongues, of black tongues.

Finally things began to settle down, the smoke to dissipate. Little by little, I came back to myself and realized that I must have been asleep for a long time. I awoke.

CHAPTER V

I opened my eyes. Beside me sat a very pretty and tearful young woman who was overcome with joy to see me conscious. She embraced me, she kissed me and wept, apparently with happiness. I could not speak. I did not understand what I was seeing and hearing. In the first place, I had never seen this young woman in my life. Neither had I ever seen the room or the furnishings around me.

No, I had never seen them. I was sure of that. Nevertheless, in

Indeciso e inerte estaba cuando testificó la primera testigo por mi defensa. Su testimonio fue aún más desolador. Ella estaba diciendo que yo no estaba loco, ¡que tenía dos cabezas! Esto me aturdió —especialmente cuando el jurado empezó a cantar y a azotar "¡Tiene dos cabezas!" Luego, "¡Cortarle una, cortarle una!" Quise defenderme pero nadie me hizo caso. Nadie me entendió, ni yo mismo me entendí. El juez vino corriendo con un espejo y me lo dio. ¡En efecto, tenía dos cabezas! Una de ellas era la mía; la otra era la de mi padre. Me desmayé.

Flotando en nubes de humo negro subía y bajaba y no sabía nada. Sólo oía el chasquido de lenguas largas, de lenguas negras.

Por fin las cosas empezaron a asentarse, el humo a desvanecerse. Poco a poco empecé a sentirme y a conocerme, a darme cuenta que quizá hacía mucho que dormía. Desperté.

CAPITULO V

Abrí los ojos y vi una joven muy bonita y muy llorosa que se llenó de alegría al verme restablecido. Me abrazó, me besó, y lloró, de gusto parecía. No pudo hablar. Yo no podía comprender nada de lo que veía y oía. En primer término, yo no había visto a esa joven jamás en la vida. Tampoco había visto el lugar ni las cosas que me rodeaban.

No, no los había visto. De eso estaba seguro. Sin embargo, ella

some vague, inexplicable manner, the woman and the surroundings were familiar. I wanted to ask a thousand questions, but I could not. I did not have the strength. I could only watch and listen, while I struggled against a numbing drowsiness that drifted over me. Then I fell asleep.

My sleep was long and deep like that of a child. Without any worries. When I awoke, I was alone. I felt very much refreshed, as if I were newborn, as if I were not the same man as yesterday. For several minutes, I took a voluptuous pleasure in the sensation, stretching and turning over and over. But the mystery of the unknown young woman and my strange surroundings sliced abruptly into my enjoyment.

Once again, I stared at the furniture in the bedroom in which I lay. Once again, I had to conclude that I had never seen those furnishings, but that they were not completely unknown to me. It was as if at some time I had dreamed that house, as if I had dreamed that girl all my life. How could I explain all this? And if I did not belong here, where did I belong? The girl thought she knew me, even loved me. Who was she? Who was I? Why was I so happy to be here? Why did this happiness bear nuances and vague echoes of past misfortune, of future misery?

I was considering all this when the girl came back. I tried to speak, but I couldn't. It was not necessary. Smiling happily, she spoke to me.

"Oh, how you frightened me! Thank God. . . ." Emotion choked her. She sat down on the edge of the bed and stroked my forehead gently. Her eyes, overflowing with tears, looked at me with ineffable tenderness. I recognized that look, but I could not identify her.

y todo lo que ahí había me era familiar, de una manera vaga e inexplicable. Quería hacer mil preguntas, pero no podía, no tenía las fuerzas. Sólo podía ver y escuchar mientras luchaba con un sueño pesado que me quería dominar. Me dormí.

Mi sueño fue largo y profundo. Como el de un niño. Sin preocupaciones. Al despertar me encontré solo. Me sentía muy refrescado, como si hubiera acabado de nacer, como si no fuera el mismo de ayer. Por unos momentos gocé voluptuoso la sensación, estrechándome, dándome vueltas. Pero luego el misterio de la joven desconocida y de mi ambiente extraño cortó mi sensualidad repentinamente.

Una vez más me fijé en los muebles de la alcoba en donde me hallaba. Una vez más tuve que concluir que nunca los había visto pero que no me eran del todo desconocidos. Era como si alguna vez había yo soñado esta casa, como si había soñado a la muchacha toda la vida. ¿Cómo explicarme todo esto? ¿Y si yo no pertenecía aquí, dónde pertenecía? La muchacha creía conocerme, quererme. ¿Quién era ella? ¿Quién era yo? ¿Por qué me llenaba de alegría al hallarme aquí? ¿Por qué tenía mi alegría tonos y ecos vagos de desgracia pasada, de desgracia venidera?

En esto estaba cuando la vi entrar. Quise hablar y no pude. No fue necessario. Ella, sonriendo toda, me habló.

—¡Ay qué susto me diste! Gracias a Dios . . . —La emoción le robó la voz. Se sentó en la orilla de la cama y me acarició la frente suavemente con la mano. Sus ojos sumergidos en agua mansa y rebosante me miraban con ternura inefable. Conocí la mirada pero no la identifiqué.

"How long did I sleep?" I asked. I was completely disoriented, unable to say anything else.

"Three days and three nights. Oh, you don't know how I prayed, how I cried! I thought you were dying or losing your mind. The doctor did not know what was wrong. Tell me what happened to you. What hurts you?"

"Three days. Three days! How can that be? Nothing hurts me. I don't know what happened. My only sensation is an indescribable confusion."

"What happened to you before you got here?"

"I don't know. I don't remember anything. That is, I remember it all, but not in a coherent way. Everything is a chaos that nauseates me and drives me crazy."

"When and how did you leave Tierra Amarilla?"

"I don't know that, either. I don't even know that I was in Tierra Amarilla. I don't know. Oh, God!"

"Now, calm down, dear. The doctor does not want you to talk or get excited. Wait a moment. I am going to fix you something to eat. You must be terribly hungry."

She left me with a kiss. I lay there cherishing that kiss. Who was she? Who was I? I did not know who we were. What a ridiculous situation! Here I was in a strange house, and the pretty woman was not completely unknown to me. And I, who was I? I did not know where I came from nor where I was going. But she knew. She would tell me. I only had to ask her. But I was afraid or ashamed to ask. She was so pretty, she seemed to love me so much, and it thrilled me so to see her. Perhaps I was her husband, or her brother, or her father, or her sweetheart.

The fantastic incongruity of my situation filled me with momentary despair. I started to pray, but my lamentations

—¿Cuánto dormí? —le pregunté todo desorientado, no sabiendo ni pudiendo decir más.

—Tres días y tres noches. No sabes cuánto he rezado, cuánto he llorado. Creí que te me morías o te me hacías loco. El médico no supo lo que tenías. Dime lo que te pasa. ¿Qué te duele?

—¡Tres días! Tres días. ¿Cómo ha de ser posible? No me duele nada. Ni sé qué me pasa. Sólo veo y siento una confusión que no puedo describir.

—¿Pues qué te pasó antes de llegar aquí?

—No sé. No recuerdo nada. Es decir, lo recuerdo todo, pero no de una manera ininteligible. Todo es un caos que me marea y me niega la razón.

—¿Cuándo y en qué condicions saliste de Tirra Amarilla?

—Tampoco lo sé. Ni siquiera sé que estuve en Tierra Amarilla. No sé. ¡Dios!

—Cálmate hijo. El médico no quiere que hables ni te excites. Espera un momento. Voy a componerte algo que comer. Tendrás una hambre bárbara.

Con un beso me dejó. Con un beso me quedé. ¿Quién era ella? ¿Quién era yo? No sabía quiénes éramos. Que situación más ridícula. Aquí estaba yo en una casa extraña y la linda mujer no era desconocida. Y yo, ¿quién era ? No sabía de dónde venía ni a dónde iba. Pero ella sí sabía. Ella me diría. Todo era preguntárselo. Pero tenía miedo, o vergüenza, preguntarle. Y era tan bonita ella, y parecía quererme tanto, y me emocionaba yo tanto al verla. Acaso era yo su marido, su hermano, su padre, su novio.

Lo fantástico e incongruente de mis condiciones me llenó de desesperación momentáneamente. Me puse a rezar. Pero mis

sounded hollow. I stopped. I would weep. Not that either. I had no tears. Between risibility and the fantastic and incongruous there is little distance. I don't know where my laughter came from, an inner laughter that looked out through my eyes. She found me laughing when she came back with a tray of steaming food that smelled wonderful.

"What are you laughing about, you rascal?"

"Because I am so happy to be with you. But give me something to eat before I die of pure hunger."

"All right, but you can't eat much. The doctor said that you should be limited to soups for a few days. And he is the boss. I brought you chicken and rice soup."

"Meat is what I want."

"Don't upset me, honey. You have done enough of that already. Eat your food."

"All right, I'll eat. Because you tell me to, and because if I don't, I'll die. It seems like years since I have eaten anything."

And I began to eat as if it literally had been years. But even in this pleasant pursuit, I could not free myself from the torment of not knowing the what, how, and when of this new life of mine.

"Tell me, what happened to me? Believe me, I know nothing. My mind refuses me what I need to know."

"Well, as you should know, you spent three months in Tierra Amarilla writing your book. You came back Monday. I was asleep. A cry woke me. It was you. I found you on the floor unconscious beside my bed. I tried to revive you, but I couldn't. I called the doctor. He couldn't, either. From that time on, I watched over you day and night, without leaving you a moment. I was afraid to leave you. You had such awful dreams and you said such horrible things. You shouted and cried. So much that it

golpes de pecho me sonaron a hueco. Desistí. Lloraría. Tampoco. No tenía lágrimas. De lo fantástico e incongruente a lo irrisorio hay poco trecho. De no sé donde me brotó la risa, risa interior que se me asomaba por los ojos. Así me halló ella cuando regresó con una bandeja llena de manjares humeantes que olían a gloria.

—¿Por qué te ríes, pícaro?

—Por lo alegre que estoy de estar contigo. Pero dame de comer antes que me muera de puras ganas.

—Pues no vas a comer mucho. El médico dijo que te limitaras a sopas por unos días. De modo es que escoge. Te traje de gallina y de arroz.

—Carne es lo que quiero.

—No me des más pena, hombre, bastante me has apenado ya. Come.

—Bueno, comeré. Porque tú me lo dices y porque ya me lleva el diablo. Parece que hace años que no como.

Empecé a comer como si de veras hiciera años que no comía. Pero aun así dedicado no podía desasirme del martirio del qué, el cómo, y el cuándo de ésta mi nueva vida.

—Dime, ¿qué me pasó? Créeme que no sé nada. Mi inteligencia me niega lo que necesito saber.

—Pues, como ya sabes, hacía tres meses que estabas en Tierra Amarilla escribiendo tu libro. El lunes regresaste. Estaba yo dormida. Un grito me despertó. Eras tú. Te hallé en el suelo, desmayado, al lado de mi cama. Quise volverte y no pude. Llamé al médico. El tampoco. Desde entonces te he velado de noche y día, sin dejarte un momento. Tenía miedo dejarte. Tenías unos sueños tan feos y decías unas cosas tan bárbaras. Gritabas y

must have affected your voice, because it doesn't sound like yours."

She stopped because she could not go on. Her lips trembled and she burst into tears. She seized my hand as if for support. The doubt and fear that showed in her weeping stirred my heart. Putting my hand over hers, I spoke to her tenderly.

"Don't cry or upset yourself, darling. All that is over."

"If I cry, it is because I am happy. I thought I had lost you. I don't want to live without you."

She kissed me. In that kiss I died again and was reborn. Perhaps the moments in which we live most keenly are the moments of death. For I died in that kiss in which I reached the apogee of my life. The blank past that tortured me was wiped out, the nebulous present also disappeared, and the uncertain future faded from view. I died as I lived.

CHAPTER VI

Grim days followed. The mystery of my life filled me with fear and despair. Every day I kept trying to come closer to what I needed to know. Every day I learned only enough to frustrate me further, there in that bed to which the cursed doctor had condemned me. My evasive mind still refused to tell me who I was, where I was, or who was with me.

I decided that this house must be mine, because everyone treated me as if it were. I also reached the conclusion, because of her caresses and the tenderness with which she cared for me, that

llorabas. Tanto que quizá te afectó la voz, porque tu voz no suena como la tuya.

Se detuvo porque no pudo continuar. Los labios le temblaban y los ojos le lloraban. Me cogió de la mano como para sostenerse. La duda y el miedo que se le asomaban entre las lágrimas me volvieron a emocionar. Poniedo la mano sobre la suya le hablé con ternura.

—No llores ni te apenes ya, querida, que ya todo eso pasó.

–Si lloro es de alegría. Es que creía que te perdía. Es que sin ti no puedo vivir.—Y me besó. En ese beso me volvía a morir, y volví a nacer. Quisá los momentos en que más se vive son momentos de muerte. Porque en ese beso en que subí a la cima de la vida, dejé de vivir. Ese pasado nulo que tanto me atormentaba dejó de existir, mi actualidad nebulosa también desapareció, y mi futuro incierto se perdió de vista. Morí que viví.

CAPITULO VI

Los días que siguieron fueron un suicidio. El misterio de mi vida me llenaba de temor, de desesperación. Cada día trataba de cerciorarme más de lo que me hacía falta saber. Cada día descubría sólo lo suficiente para frustrarme más, allí en aquella cama a donde me había condenado el condenado médico. Mi inteligencia esquiva aun se negaba a decirme quién era, dónde estaba, y quién estaba conmigo.

Deduje que esta casa debía ser la mía porque todo el mundo me trataba como si lo fuera. También llegué a la conclusión que la

the lovely woman whose name I did not know must be my wife.

I did not dare to ask her name. Nor to tell her my intimate fears and doubts. I had come to love her with an affection as deep as it was simple, a love almost childlike in its intensity and its innocence. I was afraid of frightening her, of driving her away, of losing her. I was afraid to show her the horrible things I suspected were in my heart or, even worse, the emptiness that seemed to fill it. She wanted to give herself to me completely. I held back, realizing that I had nothing to offer her. A being without being is worthless.

I began to notice a timid, silent apprehension in her. Often I surprised her watching me out of the corner of her eye, trying to analyze what was happening. Her eyes frequently filled with tears, especially when my lack of knowledge of something that evidently should be familiar to me pointed up the weakness of my mind. Finally, I decided to take her completely into my confidence. One day that seemed right for it, I confided in her.

"You know, darling, I am quite sick," I said, trying unsuccessfully to smile.

"You are mistaken in the tense. You *were* very sick, but you came out all right. In a few days you will be completely recovered and as mean as ever."

"No, dear, it is a little more serious than that. Physically, I am as well as anyone. I have no pain and I feel very strong."

"Well, then, what is the matter?"

"I don't know. Perhaps my mind."

"What do you mean—your mind? Tell me."

"I have been trying to tell you for a few days, but I didn't dare."

hermosa mujer, cuyo nombre ignoraba, tendría que ser mi esposa por las caricias que me hacía, por la ternura con que me cuidaba.

Pero no me atrevía a preguntarle su nombre. Ni a contarle mis íntimos temores y dudas. Había llegado ya a quererla con un cariño tan profundo como era sencillo, con amor casi pueril en su intensidad, en su inocencia. Y tenía miedo espantarla, ahuyentarla, perderla. Temía mostrarle lo horrendo que sospechaba que había en mi alma, o aun peor, el vacío que parecía que tenía. Quería ofrecérmele todo. Me detenía cuando pensaba en que no tenía qué ofrecerle. Un ser sin ser no vale nada.

Empecé a notar en ella un recelo silencioso y tímido. De continuo la sorprendía mirándome del rabo del ojo queriendo analizar lo que me pasaba. Se le llenaban los ojos de lágrimas a menudo, especialmente cuando mi falta de conocimiento de algo que evidentemente debía serme familiar ponía en relieve la flaqueza de mi espíritu. Por fin me decidí a ponerla en mi confianza. Un día que parecía destinado para ello confié en ella.

—Sabes, querida, que yo estoy muy enfermo.— le dije queriendo sonreír, sin lograrlo.

—Estás equivocado en el tiempo. *Estuviste* muy malo. Pero saliste bien. En unos cuantos días estarás completamente restablecido y tan atroz como siempre.

—No, chica, es un poco más serio que eso. Físicamente estoy tan bueno y sano como cualquiera. No me duele nada y me siento muy fuerte.

—Pues entonces, ¿qué es?

—No sé. Acaso mi mente.

—¿Cómo así? Dime.

—Hace muchos días que trato de decirte y no me he atrevido.

"Why not? Isn't it my place to take care of you and love you, no matter what happens?"

"What I have to say is not easy. Believe me, I love you with all my heart, and for that reason I don't want to hurt you. Listen and be patient with me. Forgive me if I offend you. I don't know what happened to me. You say I was unconscious. I did not know it. You also tell me that I was writing a book. I did not know that, either. In short, I remember absolutely nothing about my past. The only knowledge I have is what I have acquired since the day I awoke from my swoon. My past is a black night. My present is a kind of fog. My future I can't even guess. I am a very unfortunate man. I don't even know who I am! I have forgotten even that."

"Don't worry, my darling. I will help you recover your memory. You will see. Soon you will be as well as you ever were. All this will be as if it had never happened." She said it only to encourage me. I knew that.

One doctor came and another and then more. After them came the psychologists. At first, I rested my tired spirit on them and left my destiny in their hands. But after much waiting and praying, I saw that they did not know what they were dealing with. They held consultations and whispered together and gave themselves the airs of mystery and apparent wisdom so common to all doctors, especially when they are trying to hide their ignorance. They did nothing but argue and mouth Latin terms and big words that did not fit the case, such as dementia, melancholy, schizophrenia, amnesia, and so on. They bored and insulted me with questions and stupid experiments that succeeded only in exciting me. Completely disillusioned and annoyed, I dismissed them one day and told them not to come back.

One morning I felt strong enough and started to get up. My

—¿Y por qué no? ¿No estoy yo para cuidarte y quererte venga lo que venga?

—Es que lo que tengo que decir no es fácil. Créeme que te quiero con toda el alma, y que por eso no he querido lastimarte. Escúchame y ten paciencia conmigo —perdóname si te ofendo. No sé lo que me pasó. Tú dices que me desmayé; yo no lo sabía. También dices que escribía un libro; tampoco lo sabía. En efecto no recuerdo absolutamente nada de mi pasado. Los únicos conocimientos que poseo son los que he adquirido desde el día que desperté del desmayo. Mi pasado es una noche totalmente obscura. Mi presente es una niebla. Mi futuro, ni siquiera lo puedo ver. Soy un hombre muy desgraciado. ¡No sé quién soy! Hasta eso se me olvidó.

—No te apenes vida mía. Yo te ayudaré a recobrar tu memoria. Ya verás que pronto estarás tan saludable como siempre. Todo esto será como si no hubiera sido. —Lo dijo solamente para animarme. Lo conocí.

Vino un médico, y otro, y otros, y después de ellos, los sicólogos. Al principio apoyé mi cansado espíritu en ellos y dejé en sus manos mi destino. Pero después de mucho esperar y de mucho rogar vi que ellos no sabían de qué se trataba. Se consultaban y se cuchicheaban y se daban aquellos aires de misterio y de aparente sabiduría tan propio de los médicos, especialmente cuando tratan de ocultar su ignorancia. No hacían más que pelotear y magullar latines y palabrotas que no daban al caso, tales como decaimiento de ánimo, melancolía, nervios, vencimiento cerebral, amnesia, etc. Me aburrían y me insultaban con preguntas y experimentos estúpidos que no lograban más que enfadarme y excitarme. Completamente descepcionado y fastidiado los despedí un día y les dije que no volvieran.

wife came running to dissuade me and ended by helping me. Leaning on her arm, I took a walk through the house. I saw for the first time what I already knew in my heart. Every object, every picture was as familiar to me as the palm of my hand, but the secret of whom and under what conditions I had known them was beyond my present memory. Everything teased me from behind a veil that covered but suggested.

Suddenly I found myself in the living room. The first thing I saw was a large oil painting above the fireplace. I went over and looked at it with great interest. It was certainly I. Nevertheless, there were hidden, almost indefinable traits in that face that were different from those I had seen that morning in the mirror when I shaved. Then it was not I. It must be a brother or some other relative, perhaps my father. I had almost convinced myself of that when I noticed the scar above the left eye. Instinctively I felt of my left eyebrow. There was an identical scar.

There was no doubt. It was I. But what explained the tenuous but very real difference between the face in the picture and my own? There did not seem to be any discrepancy in our ages. The differences, then, could not be due to the changes wrought by years. Perhaps it was the fault of the artist, whoever he was. Yes, it must be that. The artist had not painted me well. With that thought, I calmed down and continued to examine everything. Always trying to find the secret which was denied me.

Suddenly I came upon a photograph which stopped me in my tracks. It was I, but once again it was not I. It was I without the scar. The face in the photo bore a close resemblance to mine. Nevertheless, there was something vague about it that did not belong to me. In addition, this person was wearing clothes that had been out of style for some time. I could stand it no longer. I

Una mañana me sentí bastante fuerte e hice por levantarme. Mi esposa corrió a disuadirme y terminó por ayudarme. Deteniéndome del brazo me paseó por la casa. Vi por primera vez lo que ya conocía. Cada objeto, cada cuadro me era tan conocido como la palma de mi mano pero el secreto de cuándo y en qué condiciones los conocí estaba más allá de mi memoria. Todo me coqueteaba detrás de un velo que tapaba pero sugería.

De pronto me encontré en la sala. Lo primero que vi fue un gran cuadro al óleo sobre la chiminea. Me dirigí a él y lo observé con interés. Era yo seguramente. No obstante, había en aquella cara rasgos ocultos, casi indefinibles, distintos a los de la cara que había visto esa misma mañana en el espejo cuando me hice la barba. Entonces no era yo. Sería un hermano u otro pariente, quizá mi padre. Casi me había convencido de que eso tenía que ser cuando noté la cicatriz sobre el ojo izquierdo. Instintivamente me palpé la ceja izquierda. Ahí estaba la idéntica cicatriz.

No cabía duda. Era yo. ¿Pero cómo explicar la diferencia tenue, pero real, que había entre la cara del cuadro y la mía? No parecía haber discrepancia entre nuestras edades. Entonces no podían ser las alteraciones de los años. Quizá fuera culpa del artista, quienquiera que fuera. Sí, eso era. El artista no me había pintado bien. Con esto me sosegué y seguí revisando todo. Tratando siempre de hallar el secreto de mis negaciones.

De pronto di con una fotografía que me detuvo súbitamente. Era yo otra vez pero no era yo. Era yo sin la cicatriz. La cara de la foto se parecía a la mía también mucho. Sin embargo había en ella algo vago que no era mío. Además, esta persona llevaba ropa que ya hacía mucho estaba fuera de moda. No pude resistirlo. Se

questioned my wife, who was watching me attentively and seriously. "It is your father," she replied. I did not want to ask anything more.

The fantastic thing was that my own face was a mixture, a link between the face in the painting and that of the photograph. I could not understand it. I felt myself becoming dizzy. I was led like a somnambulist back to bed, where I feel asleep immediately.

Some days later, finding me gloomy and dispirited, my wife brought me a manuscript.

"Look, here is your book. Read it. Perhaps it may amuse you and cheer you up. Perhaps it may contain the answers to your questions."

I lifted my eyes and noticed how thin she had grown, how pale her face was, how sadness had become a part of her. What I would have given to free her from the suffering that was devouring her! If I could only have said something to cheer her up, but I did not know what, I did not know how.

"Thank you, Mima." I did not know where this name came from.

I began to read indifferently. But as I advanced in the narrative, my apathy changed into something volatile and revivifying. Here, here was the key to my life! My eager, palpitating being was sensing the explanation of its existence. What was written there found a natural echo in the emptiness of my life and began to fill it with a vital resonance. So much so that at times it deafened and stunned me.

When that happened, I had to stop reading until those waves of silent sound ebbed away. I lay still for long periods, trying to understand, trying to remember, trying to synchronize the life of the book with my own.

lo pregunté a mi mujer que me miraba atenta y seria. "Es tu padre", me respondió. No quise preguntarle más.

Lo fantástico era que mi cara era un intermedio, una mezcla, entre la cara del cuadro y la de la fotografía. No me lo pude explicar. Me sentí mareado. Fui llevado, como un sonámbulo, a la cama donde me dormí enseguida.

Unos días después, hallándome triste y cabizbajo, me trajo mi mujer un manuscrito.

—Mira, aquí está tu libro. Léelo, quizá te divierta y te entusiasme. Quizá tenga tu salvación.

Levanté la vista y me fijé en lo flaco que se había puesto, en la palidez de su rostro, en la tristeza que se había hecho parte de ella. ¡Cuánto hubiera dado por librarla de la pena maligna que se la estaba comiendo! Le hubiera dicho algo que la alegrara, pero no supe qué, no supe cómo.

—Gracias, Mima.— Este nuevo nombre me vino de no sé donde.

Me puse a leer, indiferentemente. Pero a medida que me iba metiendo en la narración se iba convirtiendo mi atrofia en algo volátil y vivificante. Aquí, aquí estaba la clave de mi existencia. Mi ser anhelante y palpitante olfateaba casi su razón de ser. Lo que ahí estaba escrito halló su eco natural en el vacío de mi existencia y empezó a llenarlo con su resonancia vital. Tanto que a veces me ensordecía y aturdía.

Cuando eso ocurría tenía que dejar de leer hasta que se apaciguaban esas olas de sonido silencioso. Permanecía quieto por largos ratos queriendo comprender, queriendo recordar, queriendo sincronizar la vida del libro con la mía.

I accompanied the Alex of the book to his native village, full of love for his father, helped him cover time and space gathering information for his book. I suffered with him the frustrations of one who loves deeply and tries in vain to express his feelings. Finally, I identified with him completely. I became convinced that I was Alex.

Clipped to the manuscript were some notes that I read with even greater interest. I felt again the doubts and then the despair of Alex in his struggles with his subconscious mind. I fell back almost lifeless when I read about the night when he saw the face in the glass of wine and about the subsequent appearance of the older Alexander.

Then doubt seized me. Which one was I? Anxiously I hastened to finish the notes. Already the tremendous conflict of the author was raging within me.

I was bitterly disappointed to find that the notes were not complete—that there was no solution. That I would have to find my own answer.

Many days of intellectual upheaval passed for me. I understood things better, but I was deeply enmeshed in the tragedy. Who was I? Sometimes I thought I was the son, sometimes the father, sometimes a combination of the two. But I was never sure.

Meanwhile, Mima grew paler and paler. I did my best to make her happy. I knew very well that she often wept in secret. The traces of her dried tears dampened my own eyes. She was tearing herself to pieces for me, and I was dying for her. She suspected—I did not know what. I could not free her from her doubts. Both of us were very thin.

The shadow of my old—or perhaps new—memory rose from my conscious and subconscious suffering and began to reveal

Acompañé al Alex del libro a su tierra natal, y lleno de amor por su padre, le ayudé a recorrer tierra y tiempo recogiendo informes para su libro. Sufrí con él las frustraciones del que quiere mucho y quiere más expresarlo, sin poderlo. Por fin me identifiqué con él del todo. Me convencí de que yo era el Alex.

Adjuntas al manuscrito estaban unas notas que leí con aún mayor interés. Sentí de nuevo las dudas y luego la desesperación al luchar Alex con su inconsciencia. Quedé casi exánime cuando leí lo de la noche triste cuando se vió en la copa de vino, y la aparición de Alejandro, el viejo.

Luego me cogió la duda. ¿Era yo éste o era aquél? Con muchas ansias me apresuré a terminar las notas. El conflicto tremendo del escritor estaba ya en mí.

Mucha fue mi decepción al ver que las notas no estaban completas, que no había solución. Que yo tendría que hallar mi propia solución.

Pasaron muchos días de trastorno intelectual para mí. Me encontraba mucho más iluminado pero mucho más enredado. ¿Quién era yo? A ratos me convencía que era el hijo, a ratos el padre, a ratos una combinación de ambos. Pero nunca estaba cierto.

Entre tanto, Mima se ponía cada vez más pálida. Yo me esmeraba más en alegrarla. Sabía bien que ella lloraba mucho en secreto. El vaho de sus lágrimas secas me humedecía los ojos. Se desvivía por mí, y yo me moría por ella. Ella sospechaba no sabía qué. Yo no podía sacarla de sus dudas. Los dos estábamos muy flacos.

De mi torturada consciencia o inconsciencia surgió la sombra de mi vieja memoria, o quizá nueva, y comenzó a revelarme cosas

unimportant, fragile things, fleeting glimpses of my past. I decided to finish writing Alex's book, beginning with his departure from Tierra Amarilla.

I was engrossed in this work for several months, using my weak memory and my imagination to present the reality, or the semblance of reality, which it was my lot to see. Alex's work I left exactly as I found it, without any editing. I continued with my own torture due to my ignorance of who I am or even *if* I am. The manuscript gave me much information, but it denied me much, much more. Perhaps some day another I, like the Alex in the book, may fall unconscious, and from that beginning may spring another novel.

Mima has often wanted to read the manuscript, but I have refused, telling her that she will see it in print, that I am going to dedicate the book to her. I love her so much. I am so afraid that she will reject me as a noxious thing from beyond the tomb when she learns about the crime of my existence. Besides, like the man in the book, I feel a wild hope that my salvation lies in her, that she can give me the reality and life I need—if she does not abandon me.

But I cannot keep the truth from her much longer. Yesterday I received a letter from my publishing house telling me that under separate cover they were sending me several copies of *Man Without a Name*. They should arrive today. How happy Mima was with the news! What anguish I felt—and still feel! Tonight we are celebrating the occasion, she and I—and the one who caused all this misfortune. This person and I are inseparable. Tonight we celebrate. Tomorrow—who knows?

indecisas, frágiles, hurañas de mi pasado. Me decidí a terminar el libro del Alex, empezando con su intentada partida de Tierra Amarilla.

En eso estuve engolfado varios meses, valiéndome de mi débil memoria y de mi fantasía para presentar la realidad, o el velo de la realidad, que a mí me tocó ver. He dejado el texto de Alex conforme lo hallé, sin redacción ninguna. Yo sigo con mi tormento de no saber quién soy, ni siquiera si soy. El manuscrito me informó mucho pero me negó mucho más. Quizá algún día con otro, yo, como el Alex en el libro, caiga desmayado, y de ahí surja otra novela.

Mima ha querido muchas veces leer el manuscrito pero se lo he negado, diciéndole que ya lo verá impreso, que al cabo se lo voy a dedicar a ella. La quiero tanto. Tengo tanto miedo que me rechace como cosa malsana, cosa de ultratumba, cuando se informe de mi delito de ser. Además, como el del libro, tengo una loca esperanza que en ella está mi salvación, que ella me ha de dar la realidad y vida que me faltan si no me abandona.

Pero ya no puedo ocultárselo mucho más. Ayer recibí carta de la casa editorial que imprimió el libro diciéndome que bajo cubierta me mandaban unos ejemplares de *Hombre sin nombre*. Hoy han de llegar. ¡Qué gusto tuvo Mima! ¡Qué dolor tuve y tengo yo! Esta noche celebramos el acto, ella y yo, y el que me causó todo esta desgracia. Este y yo somos inseparables. Esta noche celebramos. Mañana, ¿quién sabe?